"Love in Havana, love found and mislaid. In thoughtfully chosen words—just those needed, and no more—Mylene Fernández offers us a magnificent gift. Her story of lost love and the difficult pursuit of literature is at the same time an X-ray of life in Havana, set in a present where glimpses of the future have not yet arrived."—**LEONARDO PADURA**, author of *The Man Who Loved Dogs* and the Mario Conde novels of Havana

"This forthright and lyrical novel tears at our hearts with the dilemmas facing its characters and their city, from a perspective that can come only from a woman writer in full consciousness of her gender. The fresh panorama of Cuban society today is painted without taboos or constraints, with a faith in human possibilities, and above all with a courage that stems from what is most legitimate and durable in ourselves."—**NANCY MOREJÓN**, author of *Looking Within: Selected Poems* and *Piedra Pulida*

"What I liked most about *A Corner of the World*, Mylene Fernández-Pintado's wonderful novel, is how superbly human it portrays its characters. They are neither political nor apolitical, and both brave and uneasy, living in a 21st-century Cuba that does not easily conform to expectation. *A Corner of the World* is about desires and dreams, and, of course, about love." —**ACHY OBEJAS**, author of *Days of Awe* and *Ruins*

"No novel I have read in the past two years has attracted me as much as this one—for many reasons, but especially because it manages to capture within its few pages so many key elements of today's Cuba."—**CIRA ROMERO**, *La Jiribilla*

"A captivating story of love, emigration, and separation in today's Cuba and today's world. Like the best of Truman Capote, another master of the short novel, Mylene Fernández gives us a cast of unforgettable characters: contradictory, complex, and human."
—**FERNANDO PÉREZ**, director of *Suite Habana*, *Life Is to Whistle*, and *Madagascar*

"*A Corner of the World* is a story of a city and its people—a love story in which Havana is the ally and also the observer of its inhabitants. To that city Marian, the main character, is our guide, introducing us to settings and characters, to their hopes, frustrations, and rejections. Some live on memories, others take to the seaside Malecón to sustain their unfulfilled dreams. To read this book is to encounter one of the best and most intimate works of Cuban literature of the 21st century."—**MABEL CUESTA**, author of *Cuba post-soviética: un cuerpo narrado en clave de mujer*

"Seductive and sensitive, written in clear and direct prose, Mylene Fernández offers us a sad, erotic, tender, and sometimes ironic tale of passion and desertion. In this story, Havana is more than a backdrop—the city becomes a co-protagonist, a confidante, a point of departure and return, and of waiting. This novel is for anyone, anywhere, who cares about what other people lose and find. It's for readers curious about the interior adventures of their fellow human beings, adventures that come with literary pleasures and an alchemy of fiction and life."
—**SENEL PAZ**, novelist and screenwriter of *Strawberry and Chocolate*, *Things I Left in Havana*, *In the Sky with Diamonds*

A CORNER OF THE
WORLD

A CORNER OF THE
WORLD

Mylene Fernández-Pintado

Translated from the Spanish by Dick Cluster

City Lights Books, San Francisco

A CORNER OF THE WORLD
Copyright © 2011 Mylene Fernández-Pintado
English language translation copyright © 2014 Dick Cluster

First published as *La esquina del mundo* by Ediciones Unión in 2011

First City Lights Books edition, 2014

Cover photograph: Paolo Gebhard

Library of Congress Cataloging-in-Publication Data
Fernández Pintado, Mylene, 1963–
  [Esquina del mundo. English]
 A corner of the world / Mylene Fernández Pintado ; translated from the Spanish by Dick Cluster.
    pages cm
  ISBN 978-0-87286-622-5
  I. Cluster, Dick, 1947– translator. II. Title.

PQ7390.F436E8613 2014
863'.64—dc23

                    2014016994

City Lights Trade Paperback ISBN: 978-0-87286-622-5
eBook ISBN: 978-0-87286-653-9

City Lights Books are published at the City Lights Bookstore
261 Columbus Avenue, San Francisco, CA 94133
www.citylights.com

For my parents, in the sky with diamonds.

For Mauricio and Pablo, in the yellow submarine.

. . . the name of a corner of the world where I would wait for you.
—*Pedro Salinas,* La voz a ti debida

The mechanic poked his head out from under the car to be-rate me for being stupid, for letting myself get taken by the mechanic before him, who had also berated me for falling into the trap of the one before that. As always in such situations, I had two choices. One was to wholeheartedly agree, which would provoke a dialogue. The other was to adopt the shamefaced expression befit-ting a victim of countless members of the guild. That would lead to a monologue.

My mother's death had made me the sole heir of a car that, while inadequate by international standards, was satisfactory by our local ones. We are not very demanding in the matter of cars. My "brand-new" 1970 Moskvich was a treasure on wheels.

"Are you a writer?" the mechanic asked.

To mechanics, writers are people with clean hands and lots of money.

To writers, mechanics are people with dirty hands and lots of money.

My mother didn't leave me any money, but she did leave some things of value: an upright piano and lots of sheet music. Her mu-sic. All I can do with the instrument is to put my hands on the keys and have them respond without much conviction. Still, out of all the objects she left that cluster indifferently around me, that piano feels the most my own.

I also inherited a porcelain table setting, silverware that's truly silver, and linen tablecloths. Also glassware of all sizes and sorts.

Endless treasures that have no means of locomotion. We take care of them all our lives, and they almost always survive us.

Also she left me a gaping void of loneliness, at the age of thirty-seven.

What's the net weight of a writer, I asked myself before replying to the question. The number of books? The number of prizes? The tally of foreign publishers? The crowd of reporters pursuing you? The quantity of gossip?

"I'm no writer," I told him while trying to understand what he was doing to the car and promising myself not to be deceived again.

I don't write stories, novels, or poetry. I don't publish books, win prizes, or get interviewed anywhere. Nobody recognizes me on the street. Nobody snipes at me. That answer, I thought, would be true.

"So what do you do?" The voice emerged from under the car, from the space lit by a crude lantern he must have invented himself.

"I'm a Spanish language professor at the University."

I awaited the indifferent "Oh" of someone who has inquired merely to have something to say, but instead the mechanic wanted to know whether I liked my job.

"No."

He poked his head out again, this time to confirm what is generally repeated here: That Moskviches had been produced by the youth of the Leninist *Komsomol* on Sundays of "volunteering."

"I teach first-year students," I added, "which means my classrooms are full of geniuses who haven't yet found out that what they'll end up learning will serve to make them depressed at the sight of a decently turned phrase."

"And how do you get along with them?" continued the interview from underneath the car.

"I think they think I'm very gray," I said as if I knew what they would answer. "I don't carry out projects with universities abroad, I don't travel, I don't know anyone who's anyone in that world."

"So what? In the end, you're the professor. Who cares?"

"You're right. None of it keeps me awake at night." That was the truth, in fact.

"The shape this car is in, you're a brave girl driving it around. It's a miracle you're alive. Look at this steering." He made that last comment for his own benefit, since I couldn't see anything.

"Yes, I'm very brave." My point was that he shouldn't see me as a damsel in distress and subject to swindles.

Brave I am not. That's why I've never written anything but class preparation notes. I'd be completely unable to come up with striking answers if I were asked about my next work in progress, or the literature being written on or off the Island, or how I manage to write with so much else to keep me busy.

Other than the sacred profession of teaching, I don't have anything to keep me busy. No animals, no plants. I have books, but they'll stay alive even without dusting. I have a room of my own and all the time in the world. In other words, I'd have no excuse for not being a magnificent writer before even composing my first line.

Those were my thoughts as I watched the decrepit Moskvich pant and hiccup at each touch of the mechanic, every time he tightened, loosened, or straightened anything.

OLGA, MY BOSS, ASKED me to come see her after class. To talk. She did that often enough, convinced as she was that she could always assign me departmental tasks. I was the only one who hadn't taken off on some ambitious personal pursuit. I prepared for class as if for catechism. During our boring staff meetings full of talk about requirements for the major, syllabi, the glowing futures of the School of Language and Literature and the Spanish tongue, I didn't let my eyes stray to the clock. And as always, I was in no hurry to go home. I live nearby, and nothing awaited me but the voices on my answering machine, my point of contact with the rest of the world.

Olga smiled maternally as I came into the office, assessing me with a glance. The severe eyeglasses on her appealing, plump face contrasted with her clothes of impressionist hues. I thought that Olga radiated vitality and serenity, like sunflowers or the sea. I smiled back and sat down.

"Marian, sweetie, it's been so long since we've talked. I know you're deep in your work the way I wish the rest of the department would be, but don't you think you ought to be projecting yourself a bit more toward the outside?"

Since I was not sure how many kilometers were implied by the word "outside," I envisioned a panorama that stretched from a modest provincial institution to the planet's most exalted gathering of Hispanicists.

"You know we're always in touch with the Writers Union, the Book Institute, and the publishing houses. Many of our professors write." Olga made a face that suggested none of them were any good. "Others do criticism or essays or study Literature for the benefit of audiences beyond their students. You've never shown any interest in that. You don't know the authors of Literature except by hearing of them or exchanging occasional greetings. I haven't wanted to push you, but lately I can't get out of my head that it's just your shyness getting in your way. So I feel guilty. If you haven't done anything on your own initiative, I haven't assigned you to do it either."

This prologue was full of truths, but I didn't suppose she had summoned me just for us to wallow in our respective guilts. Since I was in agreement so far and wanted to know what was coming, I urged her onward with my eyes.

"Here's the book of a very young writer, without any literary background, who has won a prize for debut works." She showed me a bound galley of a thin volume with an awful cover. "The head of the award committee has asked me to provide some words as a preface. The first press run will be five hundred copies, with presentations of the book around the country. The opening pages, the ones that will give the readers some orientation, will be yours. Tell me, sweetie, what do you think?"

Olga is a forceful person who has taught Literature for decades, which explains why she talks like that. What she offered sounded to me like Gallimard, the Sorbonne, and a European tour. Which is to say, it was terrifying. But I told her I would do it. At least I'd have something to report to the mechanic next time, I said sarcastically to myself.

My acceptance surprised her, but it fit her theory that my problem was shyness, not any lack of desire to step into that world. Her guilt mounted for not having made such a proposal before. She handed me the book. Its author was twenty-two and had written nothing else except a few poems—unpublished, I supposed.

On the first page, she wrote down a phone number, "Because I'm sure it would be good for you to talk with him. You'll want to ask him many things, and probably you'll be the one to present the book to the public, at least here in Havana. It would good for you to be in contact from the get-go."

The Eskimo, by Daniel Arco, went into my purse. That day my pace quickened. I walked the way a writer of great prefaces would carry a great book through a city of subways, taxis, and broad sidewalks. I wanted to get right to work. I was afraid I wouldn't be able to manage it, but the only way to find out was to start trying.

"The Eskimo" was also the title of one of the stories, which in truth was quite good. A man sunk in calculations about whether he could buy a mattress with one month's pay wandered through the city during the uproar of August 5, 1994, that gave birth to the exodus of rafts and improvised boats. He walked amidst people running and shouting, the defense of order and the yen to exercise power, the violence of the situation and the more ordinary kind. Through the roiling streets of Havana on that unusual day, a passerby walked without knowing what was going on. He went over and over his figures and sums without taking in anything else.

Though the story reminded me of one set during the Spanish Civil War, in which a shepherd searches for his goat amidst the conflict between nationalists and republicans, it still seemed quite good to me. It was written with care, especially considering that the writer was unsupplied with formal tools. He must have a grammar-teacher friend who corrects his language, I thought while making my first notes.

The telephone rang quite a few times. I heard voices leaving messages but I didn't want to stop what I was doing. At ten p.m. I decided I deserved a bottle of cheap red wine and went out to buy it.

Since my mother died, I've sold many of the things around the house to an antique dealer, at prices I suppose are quite advantageous to him. Little by little, the contents of once-bursting chests and cabinets have turned into money. Money for eating something not on the ration book, or for dressing up and sipping inexpensive wine on holidays.

I thought about calling Marcos to share the bottle.

Marcos and I were together for a long time. When we broke up, we said we needed a break. People say that to leave the door open. If you don't find someone else or someone better, you can go back to your ex without admitting you've been unable to make a new beginning.

We hadn't seen each other for over a year when we crossed paths at the phone company. I was paying my regular bill, while he was putting money into his cell phone account. After joyful hellos, he told me was involved with a Panamanian company that had to do with refrigeration and with a Panamanian woman in a less chilly way. He invited me to lunch, where he told me more about his good fortune, which I quickly associated with his having excised me from his life. Possibly he did too. Since everything went so well, we ended up making love. I told him that my mother had died and other than that everything was the same.

I think that some way or other I communicated that I wasn't

interested in change. He took me home in his Toyota and we began seeing each other between his trips abroad. Things were much better that way. His failures were no longer my fault, and my few successes did not flow from his lucky star shining on my sad self. We were no longer an upstanding couple making their way in the world, but occasional lovers for whom nothing that happened was the other's responsibility. We did better knowing less, so I decided not to call him to share the wine or the news.

Instead I called my friend the scrivener.

Sergio lives in do-it-yourself quarters on a rooftop in Old Havana. He writes by hand. He dots i's and crosses t's without his fingers ever touching a key. When he reaches the end, the final page does not glow on a screen or rest trapped in a typewriter roller, not even that of an old Underwood. Rather, he pens "The End" with a disposable ballpoint, a tiny gift from whomever, advertising some bar in Italy or Spain. He stacks up two hundred pages of newsprint paper filled with his tiny handwriting, ties them together with string, and adds them to the pile atop the only bureau in the only room of his house.

His head is full of stories. They assail him at the least opportune times. They drag him from wherever he may be, home to his collapsing chair. They demand to be written down. Sergio doesn't know what to do with all the stories in his head, on paper, carpeting the floor like autumn leaves, threatening to tumble from the top of the bureau. He's ten times removed from prize contests, anthologies, translators, publishers, literary impresarios, critics, or journalists.

He writes, and the writing relieves him as if he were easing heavy burdens from his back to the floor. He publishes in the obscure magazines of almost nonexistent towns, illegible supplements to free newspapers, magazines people buy to clean windows or wrap things up to put away.

He gets paid almost nothing but keeps on writing, without caring to learn about outlets that pay nine thousand euros for a story or about the people who receive such largesse. Book launches and panels that mean airplane tickets, lodging, and tourism in places one would die to visit. Residencies in European castles, parties and cocktails paid for by a foundation. Bright lights, tinsel, and sequins. Fame and fortune, that marvelous duo of soft chords and resonant blessings, neither know nor care that in an improvised penthouse with a view of the sea someone goes on making literature because he has no other choice.

We opened the bottle, and I told him I'd make dinner. He accepted with the proviso that he would buy the ingredients. This time I couldn't talk him out of it. He came back with all the makings for a good pasta dish and then, happily, told me why.

"I've got a job as a letter writer, like that guy in García Márquez. Well, only less romantic. The girls in my neighborhood have lots of international romances. They need to compose siren songs to attract their men across the sea, who now come in airplanes instead of boats. I write love letters for them."

"Love in this city. Under the blue and orange sky of the Malecón," I intoned with some sarcasm. "Endless evenings that commence in restaurants, continue in discos, and conclude in rented rooms with air conditioning and lamps that switch off when you touch them." We nodded in unison, knowing that our love affairs had never been like that.

"They show up and tell me their stories. Some have fallen in love with the guys, some with the life they're going to have. The rest are just calculating whether it will turn out to be a good investment. I transmute all that into love. Which, after all, is at the base of everything. Love of adventure, of the desire to leave, of eating delicatessen or owning a car, of going out shopping and becoming the mainstay of the rest of the family who are still here." He told me all this as we ate.

"At first I was doing it for free, but they insisted on paying me with presents or money. Some have gone, by now. They call or stop by when they come back for vacation. Others are still here, and they introduce me to their girlfriends who need the same thing. It seems like steady work … and no meetings." That was his explanation. I felt my pasta had turned out pretty well for a change.

While I did the dishes, Sergio read the first story in the book. He thought it was good. He remembered the Spanish tale I mentioned, but didn't see much similarity between the two. He didn't take the preface too seriously.

"You'll do a good job. I'll read it when it's done."

MARCOS CAME OVER TO show off his good fortune under the pretext of sharing it with me. He brought flowers, handing me a slender bouquet that seemed to have been picked from a meadow in some other latitude. It's amazing, I thought, how even the flowers priced in dollars are better. These served as advance guard for a box of chocolates, which meant he was in condition to offer gifts both luxurious and impersonal. I don't like chocolate, and my preferred flowers are white daisies of the "he loves me, he loves me not" variety. I thought Marcos would remember that, but I savored the fact that he didn't. It meant I could have the advantages that came with still knowing who he was, along with those that came with him barely remembering me. So he's both a known quantity and a stranger, I said to myself as we got into bed.

As important as the steps before making love are those you carry out when you're done. Smokers have it easiest: They light up and look at the ceiling. Fleeting lovers look at their watches and hurry up their departures, faced with the distress or indifference, whether real or feigned, of their partners.

Marcos didn't smoke. His new girlfriend lived in the Isthmus of Panama and was, in truth, quite busy. She was not the type to call her boyfriend for no reason or at an inappropriate time. So we'd begun to invent our own epilogue when my telephone rang.

Marcos gestured that I should ignore it, but we followed each successive ring and then the red blinking light of the answering machine. We heard a female voice saying, "Sounds like no one's home," and then a click. No message.

"One of your students," he declared. He made a business call, canceled a meeting, and told me to choose where I'd like to go out to eat. Next up, we started talking politics.

MARCOS'S FAMILY HAS A beautiful house in Miramar, the city's most aristocratic neighborhood.

On my first visit there, I was greeted by his mother, the empress of savoir faire. Perched on the couch, she jiggled her bare feet like a teenager and bobbed her head frequently, showing off one of those "careless" hair styles perfected in hours with a hairbrush before the mirror. She couldn't stop talking. She was intent not on finding out who I was but on telling me about herself. She was charming and complained about everything.

It was so hard to find people who did things well these days. People who could clean a house without making noise and breaking the nice things. People who could restore paintings or keep up a yard without making a mess of the thing or charging a fortune for it.

Later that night, Marcos told me her true story while we ransacked the refrigerator, in love and ravenous, trying not to make noise.

Marcos's grandmother had been the maid in this house, whose owners' claim to fame had been introducing Walk–Don't Walk signals to Havana. They'd dreamed of widening the Malecón's sidewalk so as to fill it with bistros, umbrellas, and people watching the late-model cars speed by rather than the eternal sea. They'd attempted to install Walk–Don't Walk signals on that historic drive, but the Congress had declared that it was an "express route" and the normal traffic lights were obstacles enough. The Congress was being stingy, but the owners knew by then how money talked inside its halls.

Marcos's grandmother, whose forebears had immigrated from

La Gomera in the Canary Islands, married the chauffeur, son of immigrants from Asturias, who piloted the owners' Cadillac.

Marcos's mother was born in the house. That is, she was born in one of the rooms above the garage, which was across a patio from the mansion itself.

She grew up within those gates, because there were no other poor children in the neighborhood and she couldn't play with the rich ones. She spent her childhood watching the owners' pampered son break toys, cars, and the hearts of girls dressed in expensive clothes who made dates for the *Country* and *Yacht Club* and spent *weekends* in Miami or Varadero.

Meanwhile, she finished junior high. Commuting to a distant and problematic school, she studied hard and tried to believe the rumors about students protesting against the many abuses and about bearded young men who were seizing territory in the mountains and risking their lives so that people would be happier. Her parents never talked about politics. They were poor, which had to do with economics rather than ideology, they said while serving the employers with lowered eyes and expressing gratitude for cast-off clothing, leftovers from dinner, and cheap gifts.

By the opening months of 1961, the owners had grown tired of blacks, slogans, and the fact that their plan for bistros on the Malecón had been declared an example of "prostituting the city" and exiled from any place in Havana's future. The neighborhood was emptying. Every day, Cadillacs, Chevrolets, and Pontiacs carried off those who were leaving the country with tearful eyes and heavy suitcases, bestowing farewell embraces on the neighbors who would follow soon after to the same destination: Miami. "We'll be back," was the shared hope that punctuated each of these farewells.

Not long after, amidst ebullient public celebration, other people armed with bulging key rings came to remove the NO ENTRY signs they themselves had put in place. They opened up houses and took inventory, declaring that the furniture would pass

23

into the hands of Goods Recovery and the houses to the Urban Reform.

From then on, new families began to arrive. They brought, in turn, their relatives from places with unpronounceable names. They sang battle songs, danced all night long, hung flags and banners, and insisted on calling their new neighbors *compañero* and inviting them to meetings, Sunday morning work details, and rallies for the purpose of insulting the Americans, criticizing the rich, and declaring that anyone who didn't want Socialism could get the hell out.

The owners of the house were resistant. They knew some people in the new government, and had even, during the previous one, once bought some underground bonds to finance a plan for university autonomy. Something told them that all the ferment would die down and things would resume their old course. They kept to themselves and spent a lot of time on the phone with the newcomers to Miami, who called to say that things were not turning out so well there, that one had to work and work hard.

Deliberations about the family future became more pressing, however, when the son came home one day in a militia uniform with a smiling light-skinned black woman alongside him. Without asking for anyone's okay, she sat down at the piano whose keys no one ever touched and coaxed out a contradance tune. The son accompanied the pianist by drumming on the piano bench and on her thighs.

A few months later, these last guardians of the neighborhood left with no one to bid them farewell, though everyone watched the departure through half-opened slats and half-drawn curtains. The owners put Marcos's mother's family in charge of the house, with elaborate instructions for taking care of everything until the proprietors came back.

Marcos's grandparents did not dare sit down in the dining room. They ate in the kitchen on their own plates of ordinary china, and they shined the silver every day as before. Sheets and towels, tablecloths and napkins yellowed inside cabinets and storage chests.

Everyone slept in one room, the guest room, with the doors to all the others shut tight. For fear of interrogation, they didn't talk with the new neighbors, who interpreted the silence of servants as the arrogance of ownership. Marcos's grandparents didn't invite anyone in, nor did they dare to attend the local meetings for fear of betraying those who had entrusted them with so much responsibility. As years went by, local myth converted them into the owners not just of this house but of many others that had been nationalized. Though they never denied the rumors, they died still thinking of the house as someone else' property, walking someone else's floors as noiselessly as possible, and never having touched the washing machine.

Marcos's mother was twenty-two when she came back from the cemetery after burying her father in the crypt of that family which she had taken on as her own. If only she had learned to drive, she thought, she would have returned in the Cadillac and not in a decrepit bus full of common sweat and laughter.

Entering the house that her parents had forbidden her to think of as hers, her feet felt firmer underneath. She opened doors and windows, drew apart curtains, and pierced the house's museum darkness with the light of what passed for winter.

That reminded her it was Christmastime, and she dug out the giant plastic fir tree that for many years had signified this holiday for her. She spent the afternoon searching the nearly full closets for Christmas tree balls, garlands, magi, and manger animals. When she felt she deserved a rest, she strode to the bar and poured herself cognac from a very old, sealed bottle into a fine crystal glass. She sat in the most comfortable armchair, the one for drinking and reading the newspaper. Happiness enveloped her.

Not only the Christ child was born on this Christmas Day. Marcos's mother took the opportunity to invent her past and plan her future. Since finishing junior high she'd done nothing much, but she had read the papers, watched the news, and kept up with what was happening. And she knew how to sew, which in the Cuba of the 1960s was a quite important thing.

Setting up shop in front of a closet holding the clothes of the absent family while scanning the pages of the fashion magazine *Vanidades*, she devoted herself to making use of every inch of expensive fabric she found.

Over the course of the next several weeks, Marcos's mother crafted a magnificent wardrobe of clothes made to measure for herself. She figured that stuffing the toes of shoes with cotton was not a great sacrifice if it allowed her to be elegantly shod in colors that matched those of the great variety of pocketbooks. The mirrors showed her off as tall and slender, with the face and expressions of a young lady pampered by life. She decided it was time to venture forth and play her cards.

Transferring formal ownership of the house into her name was simple. She had all the paperwork required by the Revolution to make her the proprietor of the place where formerly she'd been only a servant. All the objects in the house now belonged to her by virtue of the change in the order of things, a change in favor of those who had never had anything before.

So the young woman who was taking care of her case assured her, a woman who seemed very young to be handling such responsibilities. "But we've got to do a little of everything, *compañera*," the woman said, smiling. "I'm from San Luis, in Oriente, and here I am doing my part. Nighttimes I'm taking a prep course to study political economy. There's opportunity for all, and you should take advantage of it while you're still young, and so pretty too."

Marcos's mother did not let such counsel about opportunities, youth, and beauty fall on deaf ears. This was a city in which women wanted to stay up-to-date and improvised a thousand ways to do so, yet fashions increasingly came only in magazines and photos from Florida.

Marcos's father, meanwhile, had been studying commerce so

as to take charge of his own father's business, a print shop that turned out everything from postcards to billboards. Though it was only a small family business, they had done well and lived well. Marcos's father learned the value of work in forming ties among men, and the value of making an honest living without exploiting anyone else. When the laws of the Revolution came to rest upon private business, Marcos's grandfather turned the print shop over, content to be contributing to the patrimony of a society that enshrined the principles he had taught his sons.

That same enthusiasm led Marcos's father to abandon the study of commerce and put his knowledge and self-discipline to work as the Revolution might require. He built dams, cut cane, installed telephones, planted coffee, wrapped chocolates—all of which culminated in his being named Cuban consul to Francisco Franco's Madrid.

Marcos's mother came into his life in time to become a consul's wife. Setting foot on an airplane for the first time, she stepped off it in Europe. She saw Las Meninas, the Alhambra, and the Sacred Family cathedral. She ate *turrones* and Iberian ham, drank Asturian cider and Catalonian sparkling wine, and drove a SEAT 600. She shopped in prestigious department stores, Galerías Preciadas and El Corte Inglés. She saw Paris, Venice, Lisbon. All this helped to cement her recently acquired persona of aristocrat in sympathy with the Revolution.

After six years in the front lines of the First World, they came home to find that things had changed quite a bit. Marcos's mother noted that more items were scarcer than before, and everything seemed to be Russian and ugly.

She hated Russians without exception. "They're fat, they eat oily foods, and they make horrible war movies and worse cartoons." Thus Marcos grew up in the dual world of state instruction on the one hand and his mother's on the other. At school, the Soviets were a brave and generous people. When he went home for snack, they were rude, smelly Russians. Anna Karenina was eclipsed by Emma Bovary, Kandinsky by Miró, and the Hermitage by the Venetian Academy. The Russians had nothing worth knowing about.

Since Marcos's father was very busy with travels and meetings, his mother had full authority over Marcos's upbringing. She taught him lessons about life and explained that the most important thing was to take constant and very good care of oneself.

That's why, when speaking of politics, Marcos measures social justice on a very personal scale. The country's Gross Social Product and rate of economic growth are equivalent to the money in his wallet. Peace and ecology, religion and philosophic currents have to hold their own among his moods and states of mind. The world's velocity is measured on his speedometer. The planet's future looks very much like his next weekend's plans.

I GOT TO THE classroom and sat down to wait for the students while reviewing my lesson plan. Once when I'd been five minutes late, they had escaped under cover of the claim that they had waited the stipulated fifteen minutes but I had not not appeared.

I watched them drift in little by little, like words divided into syllables, while I reminded myself that I too had once been a beginner and that first-year students pride themselves on their expertise like no others. They feel very special. What matters most to them is the fact of having made it this far, not what they have left to accomplish here.

But any classroom, of course, is like the vineyard of the Lord. You've got those who want to show they know everything, those who approach the professor's desk every day to say something, anything, so that I'll remember them when it comes time for me to grade exams. You've got the shy, smart ones, the snobbish stupid ones, and the snobbish smart ones.

Like a good shepherd, I learn their names right away. The idea is to make them feel more relaxed, although sometimes I think they're entirely too comfortable and feel they're doing me a favor by coming to class. At least at the beginning. Later I end up liking them, just when they're on their way out.

Ana interrupted my meanderings with a smile and a question. She's tall with long hair and a pair of very dark eyes that contradict her blond bangs. She's not a beauty, but she's attractive and she knows it. She's made friends with the seniors and with some of the professors, she's a member of the tap-dancing troupe, and she expects life to provide the opportunities she's convinced she deserves. As a student, Ana is good but not outstanding.

"*Profe*, are you writing the preface to *The Eskimo?*"

"Yes I am. Do you know the author?"

Bingo. That was the question she was fishing for.

"We've been going together for a few weeks now. Daniel is a very intelligent person and we're doing really well. He's working on a novel with a terrific plot."

The classic young girl dazzled by her bohemian lover. I smiled at these unrequested confidences.

"What do you think of the book? Do you like it?"

"On the whole, yes. I was thinking, in fact, that I ought to call Daniel Arco soon and have a chat with him."

"We called you a little while ago, but the machine picked up and we didn't leave a message. He's very interested in meeting you."

"I'm interested in meeting him. I'll let you know when, so you can try to set it up." I got to my feet to suggest that the quorum for a class had finally assembled.

Ana went happily to her seat. She wouldn't pay the least attention, I thought, because she'd be busy thinking of the good news she could carry to her writer boyfriend. But I decided against letting her savor that expectation, and instead made her work like the rest of the class. I always tell myself I'm doing this for their own good, but I know I'm denying them their time to dream and sentencing them to the here and now of a boring afternoon of dead and buried Literature. I'm the professor, after all.

The next day I handed Ana an envelope.

"Give this to Daniel Arco. It includes the date of a possible meeting. If he agrees, he should send me a message through you, or call me at home."

Ana took the envelope and noted that it was sealed. I didn't like having a student in the middle of this. I would have preferred for this new period in my life not to have any witnesses from the previous era, but if Daniel Arco was sleeping with my student, there was nothing I could do about it. Above all, I couldn't do anything about her finding his beginner's contribution to Literature to be so marvelous.

MARCOS AND I BECAME lovers again after living together and then separating. What was most strange was how the success of the new relationship stemmed not from what we knew about each other but from what we had let go of. We could evoke the past the way one remembers scenes from old movies. Neither of us wanted more. Marcos, because he had organized a future that had no room for me. Me, because I didn't think about the future and I had never even organized our past.

The phone rang, and Marcos reached for it. When I stopped him, he laughed. He was amused that I didn't want him announcing his presence.

It was Lorena, my oldest friend. Lorena hates talking to the answering machine, so her opening paragraph is always the same, with minor variations.

"Do me a favor, move your ass and pick up the goddamn phone. I bet you're standing right there like an idiot, not answering. By now you know it's me and not some pervert making indecent proposals, which would actually be good for you considering how dull your life got thanks to that guy you were tied up with. I know perfectly well you're sleeping with him again, as if he had the only available dick in this town where what everybody does best is fuck. Whatever. Call me when you can."

Marcos laughed again, because he'd long ago given up on

making an ally of Lorena. While we were together he had tried win her over by all possible means until one day she'd yelled at him that he was such a phony in every way, she was sure he was the only man in the world who faked his orgasms. His response was Aesopian: He said she toiled like the ant and would starve like the cricket.

Lorena is a painter and sculptor. To Marcos, that means a fool with no future. He's convinced that art is something that no one with a modicum of intelligence should pursue today. The *Mona Lisa* and the *Garden of Earthly Delights* have already been painted, *La Traviata* and the *Mass in C Minor* already composed. Ditto for *Hamlet* and *Uncle Vanya, Don Quixote* and *Remembrance of Things Past*, although those who make Literature receive a bit less disdain. To him they're minor characters on life's journey, over-interested in the curves of the road rather than concentrating on the pot of gold at the end. Now that his goal is in sight, he views artists with pity disguised as tolerance.

From the answering machine, we heard Lorena renew her attack:

"I know you're there, cavorting with that clown dressed up in dollars. I hope you'll open the door for P.T., because I sent him over with my latest paintings that need someplace to dry. I've got no more room, and no way to protect them from the kids and their games."

Marcos's tolerance, the mask of his pity, promptly shut down. He made an ugly face, chastising me for splashing around in the same shallows as ever, stagnant puddles that would never turn into anything else. He dressed in silence. He gathered up the things that keep him company these days: his laptop, cell phone, tie, and briefcase. He set off, with the White Rabbit's hurry, for the rest of the world.

LORENA HAS ALWAYS HAD her finger on the pulse of Havana. When we were young, she was the trendsetter and tastemaker every Saturday night. Now her house is like the main square of some *città vecchia*, an obligatory stop in which to see and be seen.

She has a convivial talent for gathering people around her, making decisions for others without causing to them to feel compelled. In her orbit, everyone feels comfortable and relaxed. She knows how to get the right people together, introduce them, and get them talking. That she didn't become a diplomat would be a real loss to the nation if she weren't so foul-mouthed as well.

When she was a girl, she'd spend hour after hour drawing circles and arrows, comets and tails in red, blue, and black. Suns, moons, and cockroaches. Her mother never showed the drawings to anybody. She didn't sign her up for art courses or get her a good box of colored pencils. She waited patiently for Lorena to grow out of this phase and take up some serious pursuit. But Lorena went on painting, sculpting, and printmaking, with such seriousness that her mother began to leaf through books about art. Her lack of interest in her daughter's precocious works morphed into fanatic devotion. She began to notice traces of Giotto and Hieronymus Bosch, or was it Klee and Miró?

Lorena's first husband set off one Sunday morning to play dominoes with his friends in Old Havana while she was shaping clay into a new David, which she called David Revisited, with a penis more in keeping with his stature. That night, as Lorena gave up this attempt and decided that Michelangelo had in fact known what he was doing, her husband called to say he was still playing dominoes and drinking beer with his friends, only now they were in Florida, so she shouldn't expect him home. Since then there's been no further word from him. We always joke about how his game is going—and hope he's losing it.

Her next husband was a depressed psychoanalyst who had, in addition, a penchant for biorhythms, astrological charts, Hirschman grids, and energy pyramids. Hewing to so many doctrines as guides for life had robbed him of even the slightest freedom of action. Making love became a sort of Kabala located somewhere in chaos theory and dependent on variables such as the Zurich stock exchange index and Chechnyan election results.

He enrolled in a course in Lacanian Anguish which then became his chief preoccupation. Any attempt by Lorena to make him laugh was treated as a boycott of his central concerns. He sought out communication with his fellow anguishees around the globe and became fascinated by the high suicide rate of Scandinavia. Finally he got in touch with a Norwegian philosopher who responded with some interest to the experiments he carried out on himself. The Norwegian man proposed a trip to the fjords to see how he would react to an absence of sun. He went, his depressions lifted, he fell in love with the Norwegian, and off they went to Australia to go surfing so as to demonstrate the importance of physical exercise in the freeing of endorphins and the maximization of libido.

Lorena paints, spoils her children, curses everything, and has a heart of gold. Also two hands and a new husband of the same quality. This husband is called P.T., for Pleasedtomeetyou Tellmegoodbye.

P.T. became obsessed with travel after an event that left a lifelong imprint on him. This event occurred in May of 1968, when he was ten years old. At that time, the rest of the world was just something the adults in his household paid attention to each night on the TV news.

His aunt and uncle were happy in the possession of many things, including their son, who was the most important to them and to P.T.

P.T. and his cousin never fought. They shared everything with a generosity never possible among siblings, and they defended one another in and out of school as if each were simultaneously the master and the samurai in the pair.

Every Sunday, P.T.'s aunt and uncle planned an outing with straw picnic baskets, checkered tablecloths, and a store of jokes the uncle had collected during the week.

This time, P.T. was not invited. They said the expedition would require getting up very early, that it was a very long and tiring ride. They promised that next time he would come along for sure.

Stubbornly refusing to be left behind where a Sunday without his aunt and uncle might as well have been a Monday, P.T. stayed up all night watching the cuckoo clock.

The wooden bird came and went many times, but when P.T. fell asleep for what they call "just a blink of the eye," the Chevrolet carrying his aunt and uncle and cousin took off for a Sunday without him.

On Monday there was a math test at school. P.T. waited for his cousin so he could whisper the answers to him as always. In return, he would get valuable information about syllabification and iambic pentameter. But his cousin failed to appear, and when the teacher asked, P.T. said only, "I don't know, I didn't see him yesterday." He can still feel that sensation of being ready to burst into tears.

P.T.'s cousin didn't come to school the next day or the days that followed, and P.T. passed the Spanish exam by the skin of his teeth. So the teacher put it, drawing exclamation points in the air with the effect of public embarrassment and a private sense of discredit.

P.T. didn't ask where his cousin had gone that early Sunday morning, or when he'd be coming back. A year later, the first photo arrived, taken on a beach. His cousin was taller, fatter, and pinker. His aunt and uncle were also fat and pink, as was the car. The photo was signed and dedicated by his cousin in misspelled Spanish with English words mixed in.

After that P.T. applied himself to Spanish in school so as to be able to pass tests without his cousin, and to English on his own so as to be able to stay in touch. He never denied that they corresponded frequently or that his room was full of photos showing how his cousin grew bigger and fatter as if consuming some magic potion, perhaps in the form of hamburgers in buns.

Whenever he had to fill out any kind of official form, it always contained the questions, "Do you have family in the United States?" "What is the exact relationship?" and "Do you maintain communication with them?" P.T. always wrote "yes." He was never named a vanguard student, never received a good conduct medal, and never was selected to join the Young Communist organization, the school band, or the basketball team. When he finished high school, the laws changed. Those who had departed could come back to visit those who had stayed. They brought pounds and pounds of clothes and shoes with them on the plane, and then they bought electric fans and tape recorders in special stores. Nonetheless P.T.'s aunt and uncle declared that their permanent departure precluded visits to the Island, because they didn't want their money going into the hands of the communists. So they never came back.

From that far off Sunday onward, travel became P.T.'s obsession, whether in *The Arabian Nights* via magic carpet, in Salgari's *King of the Sea*, or in Jules Verne's *Rocket to the Moon*. P.T. filled his bedroom with maps. Thanks to his curiosity to know or imagine what might lie across the sea that surrounded every inch of his Island, he became very well read. Speculation about his future career centered on possibilities that matched this desire: seaman, ambassador, astronaut.

But the curious fact was that his restlessness died down as soon as he reached the shores of the endless beach that surrounds us. It was enough for him to be at the borders, the edges, the limits where farewells and welcomes take place. After getting a degree in transportation engineering, he took up the following jobs:

Ship's pilot, which meant guiding freighters, cruise ships, and tankers in and out of Havana's harbor, through the channel between the fortresses of El Morro and La Cabaña, and along the coast paralleling the Malecón. Knowing that on the ship he piloted, many were marveling in the manner of new arrivals, or expressing relief in the manner of those who choose to leave.

Air traffic controller, watching over the flights traversing the Island's swath of airspace. Imagining the passengers pressing their noses against the windows as they flew.

Driver of shuttles ferrying passengers between the airport gates and the steps of the airliners. Watching them take their first or last steps on the Cuban soil.

Later, he landed a job as a guard outside an immigration office. Seated in his chair and supplied with a travel book, a bottle of cold water, and a sandwich—so as to leave his post as little as possible—he would watch all the people endeavoring to find out what lay beyond the first waves tumbling against the beach.

These people arrived at the office very early, in the wee hours of the night, to secure good spots in the line. They arrived armed with patience to wait and determination to hold onto their places and not let anyone slip ahead. Keeping order in the line was not always easy, because once the early comers had claimed their ranks they would go off in search of someplace to get a little shuteye. P.T. tried to help out, acting as judge and justice when necessary, or standing in for those who disappeared for a break, or overseeing the list where people wrote their names in order of arrival.

None of this did the trick. When the office opened for the day, the magic of that open door, the signal that the night's wait was over and the day's wait had begun, completely upset the tired brains of the clientele. Numbers changed, names migrated, newcomers appeared at the front of the line or the top of the list. Everything seemed to happen in accord with the biblical maxim that the last shall be first.

Behind the arguments over who belonged where, he could hear a constant counterpoint of cries from the hawkers of goods and services those in line might desire. Vendors of coffee, tea, cigarettes, beer, sandwiches, pastries, candy, and aspirin. Typists who would fill out forms. Taxi drivers who would negotiate the *via crucis* of stamps, letters, bank drafts, identity documents, and birth, divorce, marriage, or death certificates.

P.T. carefully read the instructions posted on the wall at the entrance to the office, and then he learned more, studying the laws that lay behind these rules.

Thus he became the key figure in this place. His always friendly expression invited questions by the score. He outlined procedures, summarized steps, and explained the schedules of banks, post offices, and travel agencies where the applicants needed to go.

At the same time, he was the perfect vessel for the rain of curses directed at a set of procedures that satisfied no one. He tried to calm heated spirits, encourage depressed ones, and share the joy of those who, their arrangements completed, bade him adieu.

"What's this line all about?" Lorena asked him the day they met.

P.T. saw before him someone dressed as if she'd run out of the house in a rush, leaving her chores behind for a few moments at most. She was wearing the apron she used for painting, which displayed stains of all colors and shades.

"It's for traveling," he said with a smile.

Lorena looked in P.T.'s eyes, incapable of deceit. She gave the line another look and asked. "Where to?"

Surprised by Lorena's innocence with respect to one of the best-known offices in the city, P.T. explained that she would need a letter of invitation from the country where she wanted to go. That could be any country in which there was someone willing to pay for the costs of red tape, airplane tickets, and the expenses of her stay.

Then he recommended some far-off and least-visited destinations for which—since fewer Cubans traveled there—entry visas were easier to get. The embassies of the most-requested countries, in many parts of Europe, had by now grown suspicious of all claims about relatives, friends, lovers, or studies that provided justifications for the visa requests. These embassies were fed up with Cubans, people who were not from the First World yet not from the Third, who were neither citizens nor immigrants. People who traveled out of their own country so as to tell everyone where they went about the great charms of their home. Who lectured anyone who would listen and some who would not, drawing on their endless storehouses of nostalgia, taking full advantage of their new surroundings but always with disdainful expressions of melancholic superiority.

Lorena gazed at the line as she might at a canvas by Miró. She smiled at P.T. to demonstrate that she had carefully followed every word, and she asked one question more.

"And what do they distribute here? Visas or airplane tickets or what?"

"Passports and exit permits," P.T. answered, and once more explained the steps, rules, requisites, stages, and prices until his voice had become a lovelorn whisper on the bench of an autumnal park.

P.T. TELLS ME LOTS of things about life in exile, a term which is itself a cliché on this island which offers so many ocean views that the fever to cross the sea is nearly epidemic. But what are clichés except oft-repeated truths?

He says that those who leave always find themselves missing something. Maybe what they're missing is us. No matter how many new friends you make, there's always someone you're longing for, he says. Other places may also have very blue skies, hot weather, a seacoast, and fine heavy cloudbursts, but what they offer in terms of spatial features they lack in terms of temporal ones. Time keeps passing, corroding walls, yellowing photographs, and burying the old folks from the house at the corner—but now it's passing without you.

He's convinced that not even those who have triumphed after leaving—those who enjoy professional success, MasterCards, and high-octane gasoline—are happy. They've all left behind the most important thing, which for each of them has a different name.

Because the place that is lost is like time gone by. It holds everything we would have liked to be.

P.T. and I carried Lorena's paintings into my mother's room, denuded of furniture, where the wind rustles gauzy white curtains that lighten the blue walls. We had started spreading the canvases around the floor when the telephone rang.

P.T. knows my religion regarding the phone. It doesn't seem foolish to him the way it does to Lorena. He stood by me watching the machine, which always blinks red three times before the voice comes on.

"Marian, this is Daniel Arco. I'll see you tomorrow at five."

P.T. gave me an inquisitive look, so I told him.

"He's young and he sounds nervous," P.T. pronounced, "though he tried to hide it just now."

"I think so too," said I, but it seemed so strange that I could make him nervous like that. I almost forgot that what I had written about his book wasn't 100% positive. As always when I've got the advantage over someone, I felt the desire to give in, to be forgiving and level the playing field. I promised myself that this time my reserve would not be seen, as it had so many other times, as arrogance.

When my mother died I cut myself off and refused to admit visitors. I tried to heal myself from the bewilderment caused by so many people around me, the incessant talk about the same thing, death. Since my mother never understood what was happening to her, I, as the one closest to her, became the protagonist of this event, a sort of stand-in for the pain and despair of the person who was dying.

When I was told the diagnosis, I decided not to reveal to her that she had only six months to live, mathematically estimated anyway.

Normally we don't know when we're going to die, and we all have the right to live out our last days peacefully, without countdowns—so I reasoned at the time. No one knew my mother as well as I did. I knew that the slight improvements she experienced from time to time, which made me feel that her willpower could return her to the world of the healthy, were due to her certainty that she would be cured. So the more certainty, the faster that could happen. I don't know what nights are like for people living under a death sentence, whether in jail or in a hospital, on a battlefield or in cold, hunger, and solitude. But I imagine that every morning is a beginning-to-die, and they keep on dying until it really occurs.

These arguments convinced me. In spite of the pragmatic advice of those who repeated that my mother had the right to say goodbye to those she loved and settle her affairs, I did not budge an inch.

Instead, I devoted myself to buying things that would symbolize an imminent future in which she would regain her health and we would do many things together. To make this possible, I began to sell things that I would find hateful when they survived her, as if their inert substances were declaring themselves of greater worth than a human being.

When I bought the computer, I helped her to get up and led her into the study full of books. I lifted off the cloth that covered the machine and said to her: "Get well soon, because I'm going to need your help with this thing."

Besides charting our future, I invented a present that would make her happy, make her want to get up and stand by my side.

I told her I was writing a book.

My mother was so happy that I felt guilty for not inventing such a thing when she'd been in better shape. She wanted to help, organize my notes, pore carefully over every word of my story. I told her I didn't have anything to show yet. I asked her not to tell anyone, and assured myself I'd engendered a secret what would get us through even her bad moments with some joy. I tried to expel the diagnosis from my mind.

We made a lot of plans about my book. She was sure it would be fantastic. Thus the unwritten novel began its tentative journey through the world of international contests. The Spanish ones, offered by the cultural secretariat of every city and town. The Mexican ones, each prize bearing a splendid Aztec name. The Argentine contests, so cosmopolitan; the Colombian ones, linked to publishing houses of some solvency; the Chilean ones, multiplying day by day. Then the pathway of prizes broadened into the boulevard of Prestigious Publishers, those that offer multi-book contracts for a novel a year and hype you in their catalogues, so life acquires new shades of seriousness and commitments. You're no longer just a writer, but a worker in the world's most decentralized factory.

One day I decided to get the piano fixed. It had been a present from my father—the only trace he left for us to remember him by.

My mother had taught me a few things on it. She'd given music lessons to children more dedicated than I was. And she often played for visitors, or at my birthday parties, or to liven up the very slow Sunday afternoons when we didn't go to the zoo or a puppet show.

The piano was her private kingdom, but little by little, she deserted it, playing less and less. She forgot a lot, she made mistakes, she brought her hands to her face to brush away imaginary locks of hair.

During her illness she would sometimes sit and play from the sheet music. Those were the days on which she'd show herself and me that she was improving and that we'd have a return to Sundays like those of my childhood. But she rarely made it to the end of a piece.

Now the piano was coated in dust. I cleaned it while telling myself this was the first time I was expecting a stranger who was coming in order to stop being one.

DANIEL ARCO BOWED LOW with his right hand pressed against

his chest. Somewhere between mockery and respect, I thought. Or—as I considered his long, straight, very black hair tied into a pony tail reaching halfway down his back—somewhat like a mandarin of the empire of the sun.

I smiled and did the regular things: inviting him in, offering water, coffee, or tea. He declined anything to drink, meanwhile giving the house a once-over. He asked whether I lived alone.

Although it was awfully soon to tell him the story of my life, I found myself saying that my mother had died and I had neither children nor pets. Doing what I always do, trying to make light of my situation, to make things easier for others.

"I get it," he said as if he understood better than I. "I live alone too."

My student Ana vanished into the ether. Her dream of being a writer's lover had no place in the writer's head.

"But my house is ugly, almost pathetic," he went on. "Furnished like a shoestring movie set. That's my father's taste. The perverted genius to whom I owe everything I am." That statement contained no hint of pride. It was a way of naming the source of all his misfortunes.

The telephone rang.

"Excuse me," I said and went to the bedroom. I waited for the red light to stop blinking, which was followed by Marcos's mother's voice.

"Marian my lovely," she said with all the affectation of a Spaniard, a habit she clings to, out of her remote past. "I've stopped by a million times but you never seem to be in. Never mind. I'll come again soon and we'll have a chat."

Marcos's mother never does anything without a reason. She doesn't visit poor people with no futures. Her social life is made up exclusively of investments. I couldn't figure out what profit a chat with me was going to bring.

I found Daniel leaning against the bookcase studying my collection.

"My ex-mother-in-law," I said. "I can't figure out why she called."

"When I was a kid, and I read *The Arabian Nights* for the first time, that's where I discovered the word peddler. Ever since, I've associated it with bicycles, because I imagined it must be a guy pedaling along while hawking his wares. Later I found out what the word actually meant. So simple, but now, I don't know. I don't want to give up on the guy who bikes through Baghdad with a basketful of plantains and boniatos teetering on top of his turban. I don't want my pedaler run over by a streetcar in the form of a dictionary that clarifies the word until it turns ugly and devoid of imagination. Don't you ever answer the phone?"

"Barely." I let out a sigh that deprived my answer of the cutting tone of someone who doesn't want more questions. "Shall we talk about your book? You might disagree with some of what I wrote."

Daniel Arco was your classic erudite vagabond. He had a defense for every word, every phrase, every comma, and he told me a thousand times, tacitly, that my being unable to see many things did not mean that he hadn't put them there. Passionate and theatrical, he cited and recited the classics, postmodernists, and everyone in between. Theories of narration, plot techniques, literary history, minutiae of authors' lives. He bowled me over.

I'm not a master of rapid response. Instead I wielded my professional vices: the didacticism of the classroom, the patience of someone put on this earth to explain.

We couldn't agree. His book had no defects. It was perfect. Or, if it had defects, they were not the sort to be detected by the likes of me, an obscure female instructor. I felt I was dealing with a student protesting the grade on his exam. But to him, this was about how Literature was something beyond what I could conceive.

"Some day you'll understand, Marian my lovely, and when you do you'll have a massive heart attack." And he left. Stomping out and slamming the door.

I sat down on the couch to consider what had happened in that half hour of venting and vertigo. Never before had a stranger come to my house to insult me because we didn't agree. I was accustomed to being passionate in my responses and to listening passionately to the responses of others, but within the bounds of good manners. I thought Daniel belonged to a strange world of warriors who had stepped ashore many years after me. People who made their way not with pick and shovel but with dynamite, blowing up the rocks in their path to open it wider and more quickly.

I WAS GIVING AN exam that day. Even after quite a few years teaching, I could never enjoy exam days as respites from instruction, the way other professors did. Maybe I was infected by the students' cases of nerves, their potpourri of silence and verbosity, both symptoms of the same fear of failing.

I started thinking cynical thoughts about the adrenaline saturating the classroom, about the thousand charms of spiritism and santería that must be at work, with my name inside every freezer or every cupful of honey they employed. I tried to guess how many were wearing red underwear in honor of Changó, and how many were carefully abstaining from sharpening their pencils or were taking care to sit down from the right side of the desk.

Professors have very few advantages over students, I thought. We've already finished our studies and become what we are. For the students, it's merely the present. The future can be glimpsed as something more promising than a blackboard in the Department of Language and Literature.

Seated at the table with the stack of exams lying in wait, I watched the class file in and took pity on them all. And on myself who would have to read their skeins of pretentious argument smattered with spelling mistakes. A ceremony was repeated again and again: a greeting, more strained than usual, followed by a glance that took in first me and then the pile of papers that might contain subpoenas to a burning at the stake.

"Professor, I need to speak with you privately. It's important." From Ana this was not a request but a demand. I nodded, encouraging her to go on.

"I can't take the exam. I'm not in shape for it. I hope you can understand. I've had a very serious personal problem."

Ana had to realize that the phrase "very serious personal problem" was too vague for me to excuse her from the test. I didn't want to pry into her misfortunes, but the liturgy of my profession takes such words as "discipline," "attendance," and "examinations" very seriously, and the same goes for reasons to miss exams and documentation for the same. I assumed an expression which meant that in the midst of her serous personal problem she still might have to take the exam. That had its effect.

"Daniel and I had a big fight last night. It was very disagreeable, very aggressive, the neighbors heard everything, I'm just a complete mess. I haven't slept a minute. I couldn't even find my papers. I don't know where anything is. I know I should go back to his house to get all my stuff, but I'm scared. And my schoolbooks are all there."

Ana was the very image of pain, a sufferer out of Italian neorealism, a Magnani *studentessa*. The tracks of her tragedy were all over her face, her eyes, her peroxide blond hair.

I had to decide whether to be lenient. Or "understanding," as the students say. Was a fight with one's boyfriend enough reason to miss an exam? An exam for which she should have been studying for quite some time, not cramming the night before.

Ana could have pretended to be sick and sent a friend with a doctor's note, or a telegram about the death of relative on the other end of the Island, or a notice that she had to appear in court. Instead, she had decided to tell me the truth and hope that I would understand. Quite a risky choice.

"The first thing is that you need to calm down. Later we'll set a date for a retake." So I announced, and let her go.

There were other things I wanted to tell her, but I was only the Literature professor, and not a lovesick one.

COUPLES FIGHT. PEOPLE YELL because they lose their grip. These were my thoughts as I left school for the day, my steps following the routine of so many other afternoons. There's a lot of discussion of domestic violence: in films, meetings, analytical papers. We know it's everywhere, in big cities and small towns. It causes deaths, suicides, orphans, jail time, and psychiatric hospital stays. We know it could happen to us, yet without a case we know first-hand, what we mostly get are rumors that we choose whether or not to believe.

We exaggerate. We exaggerate our gestures, our phrases, when we defend our ideas, when we tell out stories, when we fall in love, and when we fight. Our home life is difficult. Coming home does not mean finding an oasis of peace at the end of the day, but rather another site of tiring daily struggle. Couples have a lot of problems to deal with, both together and separately, and very little space to think about themselves. The slightest agitation of the cup sends the water sloshing over the sides. But I repeat that we're a people of more smoke than fire; things are nowhere near as bad as we say. And then I ask myself: How do you know? Are you just denying what you haven't experienced yourself?

Violence is something we resort to in order to survive, to defend ourselves from the violence of others. To avoid being stomped on, so our lives are in our own hands rather than being taken into the hands of others. That's naïve, I scold myself, and yet it's often useful to explain small disputes and great crimes in the world we live in today.

Film, TV, and video games—fast cars, gun-wielding protagonists, thieves without scruples and cops who are the same—fear and threat. Faster and furiouser is the formula for success. Most effective ingredients: don't slow down, don't show pity.

Violence starts with a bus that doesn't come or a stupid meeting, and it comes to boil at home over a burnt cutlet or an attack of jealousy. So we make war in the same square feet where we've previously made love or breakfast. Once we're at war it no longer matters who struck first. We don't think through our words before speaking, but spit insults rat-a-tat-tat. We build barricades out of weakness and arrogance. There's no clarity, no sunlight, just ourselves and our anger—and the enemy in our sights. When we make war we forget who we are, together or separately. We forget the past, fence off the present, dynamite the future. It no longer matters which is Cain and which is Abel. The first hard words provoke the next insult, the shove, the blow, the tears and shouting. The slammed door, then the reconciliation, then another round, and another. Only rarely is the third time the charm.

I CAME HOME TO an empty apartment with no messages on the machine. I picked up Daniel Arco's book again. Maybe Ana was an actress of Magnani's caliber, maybe what happened last night was no fight but a party, which was why she was in no shape to answer five stupid questions about things no one could care less about, because there are many more pressing concerns in this city.

The doorbell rang, and like a robot I went to answer it. There, draped flirtatiously with one elbow propped against the wall, waited Marcos's mother. She gave me a kiss the way one might pet the neighbor's cat, sailed into the room, and plopped down on the couch with enviable grace.

Marcos's mother is nothing if not persistent, and she's a paragon among those who hold that the end justifies the means. Though we were never close, I was often the most available and patient ear when she needed someone to talk to. Her confidences were always displays of egocentrism.

"How's your car?"

Cars here are always topics of conversation. The question provokes a long answer because there's always a long story to tell. My Moskvich had originally been bought by my mother, twenty years ago, when it first became possible to buy an auto without being a vanguard worker/neighborhood committee activist/trade union leader/party member/outstanding head of household.

This process involved an office known at first as "the house of gold and silver" and later, when surprise made way for humor, as "the house of Hernando Cortés." People went there to unload valuables such as jewelry, china, decorations, paintings, and furniture. In return, they got a type of coupon that could be spent in certain stores having nothing to do with socialism or its stern rejection of creature comforts.

Alongside remittances arriving from Miami, this mechanism allowed many homes in Havana to become populated by the electrical appliances characteristic of modern life—and, at the same time, to be stripped of their mute witnesses to the life of the *ancien régime*. Families plumbed the recesses of trunks and cabinets to exhume whatever might yield them a VCR or a color TV.

The families that parted with these objects were happy to finally find some use for the "old junk" they'd held onto out of affection, habit, or inertia. Others observing the procession to this office were surprised to see how many "valuable goods" had been lurking in the homes of people no one would have guessed to possess anything important.

Objects from our house participated in this pilgrimage. The best things went, those whose cumulative value would equal the price of a used car. At first we thought we'd made a good deal, considering that we live in a city where getting from one place to another can often be a challenge. But eventually my mother concluded we'd seriously overpaid for a car that kept us chasing after mechanics who charged great sums for repairs that took days at a time and always involved jerry-rigged parts because by-the-book repairs were impossible. Little by little, the car spent more and more time in the garage under our building, abandoned to its own devices.

But a car is a very important possession, and the aged Moskvich became a sort of golden fleece for those in the trade. We began to receive offers, very advantageous ones according to those who appeared at our door.

One day a man came with a proposal to use the car as a gypsy cab and divide the juicy tax-free profits among us. He explained the mechanisms of buying black-market gas and the number of trips per day required to make it worthwhile. He left behind a set of calculations that appeared to be a textbook of integral calculus, punctuated by numbers of pesos here and there.

Another would-be partner offered to recondition the vehicle into a luxury rental that would capitalize on the nostalgic appeal of the 1970s, an epoch he said was much in vogue among European visitors. Accustomed to paying exorbitant prices to the state car-rental agencies, they would do the same for us.

The last was a mechanic who proposed a time share. He would fix the car, covering all the expenses as well as contributing his knowledge of technique and of the ghost market for spare parts. Once the car was in order, each party would use it according to our needs. We were giving this offer serious consideration when my mother got sick and the mechanic became one more voice in the answering-machine chorus. Since he knew nothing of my mother's illness, his speeches served as a kind of Brechtian distancing effect in the midst of her tragedy of injections and intravenous drips. He spoke of parts he could get, auto body shops and high-tech paints, lining the seats with leather and buying a stereo tape deck to install.

So asking about the car was a good way for Marcos's mother to begin a conversation on a noncommittal note. I recounted enough of the latest misadventures to make sure that she was not interested and had been given enough time to test the waters. Eventually, she brought up the topic of her son.

"You know," she said, "Toyotas are pretty good cars. And economical." She smoothed her hair back into place so it again seemed to have leapt from the pages of *Cosmo* or *Vogue*. "It's also true that Marcos is a careful driver. He doesn't even lend the car to Monica, and she's been driving since she was fifteen. He says driving a VW is a whole different thing, and that's really all she knows."

I considered the information offered for my perusal. Marcos's girlfriend was called Monica, she was rich, and she put up with his strictures about the Toyota.

"Has Marcos introduced her yet? Monica to you, I mean?"

"No, the last time I saw him she was in Panama."

That offered Marcos's mother a toehold for her next leap.

"Actually they're not Panamanian. In fact, they're French." This was a good thing in her book, because to Marcos's mother nothing that originates between the Rio Grande and Patagonia is any good, in contrast to everything from the Old World. "Her great-grandfather was an engineer who came with de Lesseps to work on the Canal. Then he decided to stay, and he met Monica's great-grandmother. Her father was a writer. I forget his name but you must know who I mean. So her parents were born in Panama but they have E.U. citizenship too, and I think Monica has at least one more kind. But she likes Panama even though she studied in a Swiss-American school and then Harvard."

I refrained from comment on the difficulties of being a geographically scattered multiple citizen. I awaited information on Monica's birth sign and most recent menstrual period.

"You know, I had a really hard time when you two broke up, but God answered my prayers and now Marcos is in love like never before." Everyone is grist for Marcos's mother's maneuvers, God being no exception. "You know what that means to a mother. Her family is very nice to him, and they're training him to work in the company. Since the firm has branches in Europe, most likely they'll be living in London after the wedding. Marcos is practicing his English, and since Monica's bilingual she can help him a lot. Marian, my lovely, could you make some coffee?"

Marcos's mother is good at strategy. Off I went to the kitchen to digest everything she'd told me, at my own pace. What she had told me was to stay far away from the glowing future awaiting her son by way of marriage to a rich foreigner, which would make him rich and foreign too. You couldn't let that kind of opportunity slip away. She and Marcos would not, that was certain.

I put the espresso pot on the flame, watching it as if hypnotized. I thought of telling Marcos's mother that she had nothing to fear, that I could hardly compete with a descendant of engineers who designed monumental projects and likewise of writers of note, the offspring of a mélange of nationalities who had studied in all the best schools and whose future promised admission to heaven without necessity of dying. Or I could simply say that I had no interest in Marcos, London, or Volkswagens, that I wanted to live peacefully in this city, retracing the same steps every afternoon, not considering how across the Malecón lay a world full of wonders, nor how with sufficient cunning that world could be won.

I returned to the ring carrying her cup of espresso, sugar, and a spoon. Ready for the final round.

"I'm glad things are going well for Marcos, and I can imagine how happy you must be. Will you stay here after he goes?"

"Yes. I'll go for visits, of course, but I've got my house here, and they'll need a place to stay when they come. Besides, things won't be like this here forever. And it won't do to go running off and leaving one's patrimony behind."

Marcos's mother would like for things to change, but not too much. She'd like to enjoy her house without having trouble finding loyal and discreet gardeners or servants. But if things changed a lot, the former owners of the house might come back intent on reclaiming it. In that case, Marcos's mother would become a staunch supporter of Socialism and the laws of the Revolution.

"And how are things with you? The university, your love life, all going well?"

"I think I've met someone." I tried to say this with enough mystery and passion to make it sound like a true story but rather complicated to tell.

The phone rang, and Marcos's mother looked a question at me. I stayed seated while we listened to the voice.

"Marian, I'm sorry. Could we try again, without me being such an idiot?"

I ran to the phone and, out of breath, said, "Hello Daniel, you weren't the only one. I think I ought to apologize too. Can you come tomorrow? Okay, I'll expect you then."

Marcos's mother had heard what she needed. She bade me a warm goodbye, as one does to a past that one has definitively left behind. And she departed, assured that I would be no hindrance to what was to come.

I sat down to read Daniel's book again. My future consisted of rereading the book, rethinking what I had written, re-conversing with Daniel, and rewriting my words. Fixing everything up. Doing it over. As if one could achieve the utopia of a second life free of the mistakes of the first.

Marcos would marry the woman he should have married to begin with, except that he hadn't met her yet. He had met her now because he was in the right place at the right time. And because the years we spent together taught him what life he did not want. When he met Monica, he was ready to seize the day.

Sometime, I thought, I too will have another love story to tell. Then I'll be grateful to Marcos. I'll owe him one for having taught me whom I don't want to live with.

THE WORST THING ABOUT teaching is being able to see, in each exam you read, what you haven't been able to get across to the students. Or to find out how little what you've said to them matters. So in giving bad grades you're evaluating yourself as well. Their evaluations are temporary. Yours, permanent. These were my thoughts as I graded and waited.

Daniel arrived for our second try. I hadn't straightened up the house, and I had the look of a professor defeated by a mountain of exams. He looked to me like a student approaching graduation.

"Did you study for any degree?" I asked him.

"No, I've been too busy trying too deal with the life I was given. It hasn't been such a good one."

"I don't think any of us sees our own life as much to speak of. We always think it could have been better."

Looking him over, what I saw was privation counteracted with a heavy dose of streetwise cunning. He had no mother like Marcos's to oversee marriages that lead to promenades along the Thames.

"Would you like to stay for supper? I'm not very good in the kitchen, but it will give us more time."

I thought Daniel would be good company—so far removed from my own life, barely grazing it at all. He smiled and said yes, that he was delighted I wanted to eat with him, and that, if it was all right with me, he'd take charge of everything so I could continue grading exams.

"I'm a fantastic cook. I've been making my own meals since I was a kid, so you're not taking any risk."

I turned the kitchen over to him, giving him a few instructions about where to find the ingredients for pasta with tuna fish.

"There's a bottle of wine," I said. "I expect to need it after finishing the tests."

I went back to my work, now accompanied by the quiet sound track of someone making my dinner, singing softly to himself, and not interrupting me with questions.

Daniel set the table, served the pasta, and leaned over to wish me "*Bon appétit.*"

"I could compliment your cooking, but you'd tell me that pasta cooks itself and the tuna is from a can, so you haven't done a thing."

"I'm a good cook. Pasta doesn't cook itself because the timing is important, I rescued the tuna from a swamp of ugly oil, and I stirred it well so it wouldn't stick to the bottom of the pan. Did you cook for your ex?"

"Not much. Marcos liked cooking. He couldn't stand things done badly, and the things done well were always his."

"His mother must have taught him." He took in my surprise and added, "The one who called the other day. Marian-my-lovely-I-need-to-chat-with-you." We laughed.

"We chatted. She came by yesterday. She was here when you called."

"To ask you to come back to her son, who's dying of love for you."

"To ask me to leave him alone, because he's found a rich Panamanian girlfriend and they'll get married soon, go to London, and live happily ever after."

"Oh, no. From the Panama Canal to the English Channel," he claimed in mock desolation. "Did that make you very sad?" His eyes grew serious and regarded me as if my answer mattered.

"No. Or I don't know. We'd been sleeping together again, once in a while, no strings. I knew this person existed. But that's one thing, and it's another when his mother shows up to remind you that you're a poor alternative and could ruin his life."

I didn't go on, not wanting to begin an exchange of confessions. Daniel understood.

"Why don't you finish grading while I clear up and do the dishes? Then we'll open the wine, which I put in the fridge to cool. You're a very beautiful professor," he smiled.

"When you called, it felt like someone was coming to rescue me."

"Then I was lucky to have called right then. I was afraid you'd hang up on me, which I deserved for my arrogance. You were very sweet."

"No, I think I was just nervous. Your call was providential, and I took it for a sign."

"That's why I'm here."

As the wine disappeared, so did my inhibitions. Daniel and I had gotten much closer. I didn't want him to leave, but to touch me. The bottle lay on its side. So did I.

"Look at me," he said, and something in our bodies changed. Our movements grew slower and the minutes denser. He began to whisper as if the air he exhaled carried as much message as his words.

"Forget the Panama Canal. It's a Frankenstein of locks and ships full of junk that caters to the tastes of the Americans and everyone who depends on them."

With the slightest pressure, he separated my legs and continued talking, slowly.

"Now this is the Grand Canal of Venice."

His hand began moving without touching, as if caressing me from a distance, declaring an intention.

"But not the modern one," he whispered, as his hand began exploring without hurry, "not in these times."

"We're in the Venice of Canaletto." He kissed me, stopping just at the right moment to continue describing the scene.

"No waterbuses, no Japanese tourists." He undid my hair and followed it from the roots to the ends. "Nobody takes photos or videos, but the Ponte di Rialto is already there. It's full of shops, wares of all sorts being bought and sold."

I kissed him in return. "And there are gondolas. Venice is the isle of happiness."

"You're a mystery, Marian, and ever since I got here all I've thought about is taking off your clothes and watching you moan along with me. I want to watch you sleep, naked and lost among the sheets and your dreams."

His statement was a question already answered. I didn't want to let him go, I knew that the night was just beginning, that the magic of touch would do its work many times. It was our first night and would bring all the blessings that implied.

Almost at dawn, I was indeed lost to the world, and Daniel watched me drift away.

I awoke in daylight to breakfast and a bouquet of roses.

"I stole them from the yard next door, because there's no one out selling flowers at this hour." He passed me a cup of *café con leche*. Then he got on the phone.

"Who are you calling at seven a.m.?" I asked, more out of sleepy befuddlement than curiosity.

"Home, Marian."

"Didn't you say you lived alone?"

"Yes, but last night there was someone there."

"Ana?" I thought maybe she'd gone to collect her things as she'd said.

"No."

"Some relative from out of town?"

"No."

I decided against further questions. Just because you sleep with a guy one night doesn't mean he has to tell you the story of his life, I thought, and headed for the shower.

A few minutes later he sat down on the edge of the tub.

"I think I love you," he said, staring at me.

"Sure. I'm so fascinating, I drive men crazy."

"No, I love you," and we went back to bed.

For the first time in ten years I was going to be late to work. Daniel turned the clock away.

"I can't stand to be spied on by anything one has to wind up. Okay, you want to know who I called. If I tell you I love you and want you to love me, you'll say that at least you deserve an answer to that question, right?"

"Not if you don't want to."

"The classic mature woman who knows how to win out over impatient little girls."

"I'm an impatient mature woman, so I have the defects of both."

"You're my girlfriend for the next seventy-five years."

"I won't live that long."

"I'll love you after death. I'll be a necrophiliac."

"Okay, rather than getting into perversions, tell me who you called."

"My best friend is named Adrián. He's a homosexual and he goes to bed with foreigners for money. Thanks to him, I haven't lacked for anything since we met. I owe him almost everything, including the book that brought us to this bed. Adrián has had a steady partner for a while now—a businessman, married with children, who has a company here. He bought Adrián a house, which is where they always go, but last night Adrián needed some-place to sleep with another guy he recently met. He couldn't take him to the house because the businessman has keys and comes and goes as he wants."

"That is, your friend doesn't have a house in the legal prop-erty sense of the term."

"Exactly. This new man isn't married. He's a journalist. He gives Adrián lots of money, takes him fabulous places, and gives him very special gifts."

"Would it be tacky of me to ask whether Adrián likes either of them?"

"Neither one. Who he likes is me, though he hasn't ever said so."

"To summarize," I said, from an imaginary lectern in front of a student. "Your friend needed someplace to make love to a lover whom he doesn't love, with whom he's being unfaithful to another lover whom he doesn't love either. He's in search of the highest bidder, though that's no business of mine. The great friendship that binds you to him causes you to leave your place so they can spend the night together, and you decide to come here and sleep with me and thus resolve your dilemma."

"I said I think I love you."

"Yes, noted. And you're a very knowing lover, which is a talent worth having. Like painting or playing chess. I can play the piano, I'm very good, would you like to hear? When I'm playing, I'm car-rying out an activity that involves both talent and practice. The same is true of sex."

"Of course, but not the way you think. If you play the piano well, then on top of talent and the hours sitting on your ass, there's inspiration, something that fills your head with notes, makes you feel good, safe, and at peace with yourself. I'm here because you invited me, and to apologize for what happened about the book. You were feeling sad and let me get closer than you might have wanted to. And I made love to you because I've been dying to touch you since I first laid eyes on you. I stayed because I wanted to sleep with you. Do you think there's no place else I could sleep?"

"No. No, I don't think that."

"Adrián gave me money. I could sleep in any room in this city."

"Indeed. Damon and Pythias."

Daniel stood up in a rage, got dressed, and looked at me with pity.

"We're not Damon and Pythias, Marian. We're Achilles and Patroclus. We're warriors. This city is a battlefield, and only fools like you stay on the sidelines as spectators. Good luck. Call me when we can talk about the book. I won't touch you next time. And I don't believe you're all that good on the piano."

I GOT TO SCHOOL late and the students had gone. I went to the office, waiting there until it was time for the next class, making some last corrections on the exams, and thinking.

I didn't really think. I felt. The night before, and what happened after.

"How are you coming with the book, Marian?"

Olga smiled, swathed in her brightly colored clothes. In *The Book of the It*, Groddeck says that when one person reminds us of another, we're predisposed to the new one in accordance with our relation with the previous. Something in Olga always suggested the peace of having a mother.

I told her that I'd finished the preface, but when I'd met with Daniel we hadn't agreed, so we needed to meet again.

"But it has to be quick. The presentation is less than three weeks away."

That was great news. The gods were on my side. I had to call Daniel, I had to see him, and this needed to be arranged right away.

"I'll call him from here, right now. Give me the details of the presentation in case I forget."

I needed to have someone listening so that we'd talk only about the book. Olga sat down next to me and smiled. Maybe she associated me with someone in her past too.

I dialed Daniel's number and he answered. I said who I was and there was a period of silence.

"I think I love you," were his first words.

"I'm at work, and I've got my department head here who says the presentation of your book will be within the next three weeks."

"Would you like me to tell you what I feel like doing with you?"

"When can we meet to finish up the preface?"

"Tonight at eight, and I'll bring all the ingredients for a wonderful chicken dish. And we'll sleep together again, but this time there won't be anyone in my house."

Too much all in one day, I thought when I found myself studying my students' faces in the next class, searching for traces of Daniel.

Ana came up to ask me when we could reschedule her exam.

"Ana, the best thing would be for you to write me a research paper. I don't see much point in peppering you with questions, but it would do you good to seek out information, read and process things. That will keep you from thinking about your problems." I noted almost with horror that I was in fact going to bed with her problems, and her problems were to blame for my distracted look.

"I wish all my professors were like you. Daniel called me early this morning. He asked me to forgive him. Maybe we'll get back together, I don't know."

DANIEL WAS IN THE kitchen, wrapped in an apron and armed with a large spoon, lost in his recipe while I watched him sway and sing. First we'd made love, as if the night before we had quit halfway through. As if consummation had engendered desire, the way eating can make you hungry for more. I'd never had someone talk to me so much while touching before. Filling every moment with words, naming everything, asking and getting answers all the way through.

"Shall we say that making love with you is part of my job of getting to know the writer so as to introduce his book?"

"Yes, from now on I'll devote myself to fucking all the presenters so they'll understand my words."

The preface was done. We read it over on the computer screen and burned it on a CD for me to print out at school.

We stayed up all night. I told him about Lorena and P.T., who he found attractive and funny. He wanted to meet them, to have a dinner where he'd meet all my friends. I told him about Sergio, who he proposed I call right then and there.

"Maybe we can introduce him to Adrián and they'll fall in love."

"Sergio is very poor, he can't buy your friend Armani jackets and Ray-Bans. He lives on a rooftop and hasn't got a thing to his name."

"Perfect, then they will fall in love. Adrián will provide the money and Sergio can devote himself to writing without worrying about the day-to-day. Composing letters isn't very stable work. Soon all those girls will buy computers and send emails to their foreign guys, and your friend will be out of work. You've got to meet Adrián. You'll like him, I'm sure."

We dove into each other again, came to the surface, talked of ourselves, dove again. In the intermissions, Daniel told me his story.

"My mother is black, well, mulatta, and has always been a beauty. Now she's married a guy twenty years younger, and they've got a pair of precious twins. The guy is an asshole, but she puts up with everything. My father is a Spaniard."

"So you're a modern *Cecilia Valdés*," I said as a joke.

"Not me. I'm Cuba itself—the mixture of all races, of the pleasure principle and never passing up an opportunity. When my father walked out on my mother I was too little to remember anything. Then my mother got offered a scholarship to study in Russia—some backwater school at the end of the earth—to qualify for promotion into management at the factory where she worked. But she didn't have anyone to leave me with, and they wouldn't let her bring me, so she couldn't do it after all. From then on we began to bear grudges against each other. We fought like cats and dogs, I'd cut school and hide out, she'd go hunting me all over the neighborhood with a wooden clog in her hand. People took pity on me and let me hide in their houses, but she always found me, screamed like a madwoman, called me every dirty word you can think of. When I was twelve and had finished elementary school without learning a damn thing, I went to live with my father who barely knew me at all."

"And how did you get along with him?"

"Little by little, Marian. Another day, like Scheherazade. That way you won't have me executed so soon."

I told him how I'd been raised by a single mother who never spoke of my father. My grandfather—who saw to it that I'd have a 'paternal point of reference' in my life—told me my father had left both my mother and Cuba when she was still pregnant with me. Those were the years when people left for Mexico, Argentina, Venezuela, Puerto Rico, or Spain, and maybe later moved on to the United States. We never knew which destination he chose or whether he stayed there or moved on. Nor whether he knew about my future existence when he left. The issue of my father was filed away. We all got very good at pretending it didn't concern us.

"So, you don't know who he is," said Daniel by way of summary.

"Exactly."

"Does that bother you?"

"Yes. I would have liked to have a father, but I think I felt worse for my mother. She was so alone, and I always felt guilty for it."

"That's the prudery of Bible readers, the Judeo-Christian guilt over fucking and having fun. My mother went out at night with anyone she took a fancy to. She left me with whatever neighbor would babysit, so I learned about every kind of underground business in the city and started to earn my keep helping out numbers runners and people selling contraband beef and stolen goods. I'm a delinquent, *ma chérie*."

"That was a long time ago. Now you're a promising writer."

"Do you think about the fact that any man on earth might be your father?" he asked, returning to the attack.

"Not really."

"Well, you should, because he might have ended up as who-knows-what. Maybe one day a chauffeur in a shiny hat with very correct manners will knock on your door. '*Zeeñora Marian? You fazzer haz died ahnd now you are mizzionaire.*' Wouldn't you like that?"

I laughed, thinking, Daniel is a streetwise boy who believes in fairy tales.

"Sure, okay. Then we'd be rich."

"And if you were rich, would you take me with you?"

"Sure. Where would you like to go?"

He thought this over as if we were standing at a ticket counter. His expression turned serious and he said, "First, Paris. Then we'd see what came next. My grandmother was a cancan dancer in the *Folies Bergère*." I must have looked incredulous, because he added, "I've got photos to prove it. I don't know who my father's father was, but I know he was a Spaniard because my grandmother was in Spain during the Civil War. Now close your eyes, and I'll tell you a bedtime story about all the fathers you might have."

I did. I fell asleep while Daniel held my hand and reeled off Scandinavian ship captains, Israeli rabbis, surrealist paint-ers, prisoners escaped from Devil's Island, journalists fleeing

McCarthyism, Italian gigolos, priests escaping divine punishment, mafiosi from Palermo, earls from Winchester, philosophers from Berlin, scientists from Moscow, nomads from Mongolia, Prussian field marshals, serial killers, snake charmers, and more.

WE WENT TO THE book presentation together. I didn't dare protest to Daniel that I'd rather keep our relationship secret and that arriving together might arouse suspicions.

The room was packed with people. More than I would have liked for my premier performance at this type of thing. Lots of students and faculty from the department, plus a small detachment of the curiosity seekers who show up regularly at presentations, lectures, and panels—from love of art, from boredom, or simply because these events are free.

Daniel hurried over to a tall, thin young man, well tanned, with very black eyes and hair. They hugged, separated, and hugged again.

"Marian, this is Adrián."

Adrián looked me over, made a snap judgment, liked what he saw, and embraced me. He was in fact quite handsome, with an expression both laconic and lascivious.

"This is for the two of you. A present to reward your work together." He held up a package wrapped in Japanese paper.

"No, you shouldn't have bothered," I said, saying what everyone always does when they pretend at first to reject a gift.

"Thanks, Adrián, I'm sure we'll enjoy it," was Daniel's response. He took the present, smiled, and embraced his friend again.

I greeted the professors, Olga, and the students, some of whom asked about exam results. I saw Daniel talking with Ana by the exit door. I ordered myself not to spy and, turning my head the other way, spotted Sergio sitting in a corner.

"I think you're the only one on my team at this show," I told him. "I'm nervous and want to get it over with. It's amazing how

I spend my life talking in front of students and now, though it's almost exactly the same audience, I'm afraid I'll forget everything I want to say."

"It'll be fine. Look my way once in a while."

"And then what? I mean, will you come home with me afterward?"

"Okay. I don't have any letters to write," he joked. "I hope I won't be unemployed too long."

Daniel and I sat in the middle at the head table, flanked by Olga and the editor in charge of the book. The editor smiled endlessly.

Olga spoke about the department's connection with young Cuban writers and her idea that the writers should have a place in the world of teaching, even if they didn't give lectures. The editor spoke about the pleasures of working on a book such as this and how much fun she'd had with Daniel in their work sessions. I spoke, and I must admit that in my rendition the book emerged with new virtues that had more to do with its author than the text itself.

Finally it was Daniel's turn. He said the book began with one love story and ended with another. Not its content but its process of gestation. His friend Adrián—whom he instructed to stand and present himself—had listened to the very first ideas that later became stories, believed there was indeed literature within them, and provided material and spiritual support during the period of writing. Thus the book was born. Its journey ended here and now, as it became property of the hands, eyes, and minds of the public. The one responsible for this rebirth, when the book flowered from a project into something actually held and read, was Marian—his other great love. Both of them, Adrián and Marian, the two people most important to this book, were also the most important in his life. He asked God to allow him to keep both of them close by forever. In this last part, deep emotion showed in his voice.

There was a plentiful burst of applause, and the presentation was over. People lined up to buy the book and then gathered around Daniel so he could sign their copies. I didn't know what kind of face to put on, so I hoped it just looked normal. I thought that perhaps Daniel's declaration of love would be taken as respect for a mature friend who had helped him and opened doors, but I corrected myself because in this country our first thought is always the worst one and we have trouble convincing ourselves otherwise later. On everyone's face I seemed to read the knowledge of our nights together, some with knowing complicity and others with negative judgment. I felt myself expelled from the room for a violation of good manners.

And above all, I felt used by Daniel for this clown show. Stripped naked in public without my consent. Thrown to the lions in front of the same people with whom I spent every day of my working life. Circling around the crush of flirtatious students surrounding the promising young writer, I found Sergio and told him we were leaving.

Sergio took me by the hand and said, "Not to your place. I brought my savings. Let's go a have a drink."

FIVE IN THE AFTERNOON in the false autumn of Havana is the best hour of the best time of year. The light falls on the sea and on the stones of centuries-old Spanish fortresses, on the pastel colors of capricious and tottering buildings, on inhabitants accustomed to this daily miracle, miraculous even if doesn't multiply loaves and fishes.

The bar displayed the same kitsch recently adopted by every place hoping to attract tourists. But the top-floor porch had a view of the sea, and of Old Havana bathed in orange tones. There were both foreigners and Cubans among the customers. Since the decriminalization of foreign currencies, Cubans have been recovering some of the haunts lost during the years when the possession of dollars was a serious crime and the city became forbidden fruit to its own residents. Now the means of harvesting this crop have multiplied to the point that they'd fill several volumes of a contemporary picaresque. Practically everyone has sought, and many have found, some means of acquiring the currency that opens doors to the supermarkets and bars.

"It's a relief to see Cubans again in some parts of Cuba," Sergio said as we sat down at the table closest to the sea, pushing away the used plates and dirty glasses that remained. "I told you the whole book thing would go well," he said, said, eyeing me with a fond look.

I told him everything. I wondered whether these foreigners around us, besides having money and the right to vacation wherever they wanted, might also have friends whom they could tell everything. I included details, as I always do with Sergio. On our island, we feel that good things are too good to keep to yourself. You always need to share them with someone. Good fortune exists to be cut into slices with words. The same is true of sadness. Or rage.

"I felt used. I can't shake it off. He's much younger than I am, but it feels like he's lived many other lives. Not only do I go to bed with a boy, but he knows more about everything. How could I be so dumb?"

Put that way, it sounded funny.

"Marian, you're changed," Sergio said when we both finished laughing. "You were half-dead, exhausted, you couldn't make even a tiny effort to lift up the coffin lid and look around. Now you're radiant, you've got strength—even in your anger, in this battle of teenage lovers. Your eyes sparkle, you're moving differently. Who knows whether he loves you or just knows how to make you believe it, but you're alive and full of feeling. Why run away from that?"

"I don't want to suffer."

"Hooray for you, but stupid. You can't have one without the other. Take him or leave him, which is it going to be?"

When I got back to my apartment, Daniel was sitting on the

stairs. He looked like a child sent outside as punishment by strict parents, wallowing in his powerlessness and his hatred.

"Have you been here long?" My voice sounded cold, calm, and falsely maternal.

"As long as you've been out with that friend you left with."

"That's Sergio. I've told you about him."

"Indeed. I thought you wanted to introduce me to him. Or do you only feel that way about me when we're fucking? I came to bring you Adrián's present, which he said was for the two of us though you didn't really sound very happy about that. In fact, you rejected it. Is that how girls who take piano lessons and learn good manners are supposed to act?

"It didn't seem right to me to accept it."

"Why not? Because it's stained with sin? Because it's bought with the money of an old and hypocritical faggot who paid for my friend's body?"

"Nobody forces your friend. . . ."

"You're disgusting. That's the moralism of cloistered nuns who masturbate in secret. Nobody taught my friend to play piano, and in fact I doubt he's ever seen one up close. Nobody left him a house and a car and a thousand pieces of pretty, useless junk to wander about in, while thinking that the world is in deep shit and people are neither honest nor good. He's my friend, and you don't have the right to judge him."

He tore open the wrapping angrily. Inside were three volumes of a fine old edition of *The Arabian Nights*.

Daniel buried his head in his hands and began to sob.

"I told him how that first time at your house I didn't know how to approach you so I told you the story of the peddler on the bike with boniatos and bananas on his head."

He came close and I hugged him. He was shaking. I kissed him. I stroked him. He was like a stray puppy who loses his fear when addressed in sweet, calming tones. We stayed like that a long time, seated on the stairs, while I begged to be pardoned, offered a slew of *mea culpas.* "You know what?" I told him at last. "I'm like a bull in a china shop."

"You?" That last attempt evidently did the trick. "You're so fragile I sometimes think the wind is going to whisk you away."

IT WAS THE MORNING after the presentation. I had to go to work, and I was afraid. Afraid of the students, of the professors, of Olga.

I reminded myself that to all of them Daniel was just a literary beginner soaring on the thrill of seeing his book published. A young writer full of words, grateful to everyone. To his friend and to the professor who took his book under her wing and helped him out. Just a nervous youngster wearing his emotions on his sleeve.

I reviewed the whole sequence of events, seeking some truths that could serve me as armor when I got to school.

I had read his book, that was true, and I had presented it. It was true that he had called me because of this joint project, that he had come to my house for the same reason. It was normal for us to have become friends in the course of literary talk and, along the way, to have talked of other things. It was reasonable that if we were busy working he would stay for dinner. All of which could in turn lead to the words he had uttered in the intoxication of launching his first book. Only that and nothing more, I coached myself while showering, dressing, and eating breakfast.

But my alter ego was not idle. It told me that what everyone had heard was that Daniel and I were going together and doing very well.

And now I had to confront them all. My students, in full possession of the juicy tidbit that I was frolicking in bed with someone just like them. "The professor who acts like such a saint, with her nose in the air, the one who's never absent, who never says a world that couldn't have been used in the Middle Ages. The one who's nobody's enemy and nobody's friend. The one we all thought had taken vows of chastity too!"

Ana, eighteen years old and in love with Daniel. She spoke to me to arrange a meeting for him. Informed me that they were going together, that Daniel was a genius, that she was so happy with him. Confided in me when things were going so badly she couldn't take the test. I was so understanding—or pretended to be, what a witch!—and sent her off on a boring research project so as to be able to fuck her ex-boyfriend in peace. For the rest of the semester I would still be her professor, record her attendance, judge her answers to exam questions, and preside over her life.

Olga, who gave me the book as a kind of encouragement, a stimulus to escape the routine I couldn't find my own way out of. Now she'd conclude that indeed I'd found my way out—and well accompanied, too. No sooner had she given me the first non-teaching responsibility of my life than I'd jumped into bed with a writer who could be her son. I remembered how Olga had always defended me. After this spectacle, I thought, she would no longer be so eager to do so.

And then the rest of my colleagues. I've never been very friendly with them, but that's just my shyness. I smile at their jokes. I go to department parties, where once I even danced with the semiotics professor, who's a first-class dancer. I say hello to everyone, answer their questions, do them favors and don't expect them to consider me one of the gang. Now they'll have plenty to talk about in the coffee bar, the cafeteria, and the parties where I won't dare show my face. "Marian, with that pose of a drenched cat, like she's asking your permission to breathe, so self-effacing she's barely there at all—look at her having the time of her life with the writer. That's some way to launch a book." I imagined the secretary making one of her jokes. "So anyone can present a book, it seems. Why don't we all go down to the Writers Association and ask to see the menu. Please, could you just show me the ones under twenty-five?"

"How old are you, Daniel?" I asked.

I was dressed, with my purse and hundreds of papers in my

hand. I'd grabbed a lot more than I needed, as if this were the armor I could contrive.

Daniel was still in bed, naked and wrapped up in the sheets. He'd been watching me, following all my movements. He seemed not to know whether to get up too, or assume he was now authorized to stay in my house while I was gone.

The question took him by surprise. He was expecting it but not just then, not after the previous night. He sat up and smiled. Not just at me, I thought, but at the day that was dawning, the books he would write, the future that would be very fine.

"I'm twenty-two, you're thirty-seven, and when I was born you already had your period. You were in junior high and some skinny guy with pimples was putting moves on you at parties with the lights out and the BeeGees on the record player. Is that what you're trying to say?"

"No. I'm trying to say that when I'm fifty you'll be thirty-five."

"And we'll still be together, and I'll cheat on you with a twenty-year-old. What do you want? Do you want to leave me because you'll suffer fifteen years from now? Or because what you want is a husband, kids, a dog, and lunch with your in-laws on Sunday?"

He laughed and knelt down theatrically before me, with his hand on his heart.

"I swear, you'll be my corpse of a girlfriend and I'll descend into hell to get you back."

I RUSHED INTO THE department office like someone with a lot to do and no time to talk. The secretary was glued to the computer, checking emails from her internet boyfriends.

"Hi Marian," she said with a big smile. "When you slipped out yesterday, we thought the kid was going to have a heart attack. He went around asking everybody where you had disappeared to. He gave the complete cold shoulder to a reporter who wanted to ask him questions. Did you see him later?

"Yes, he came over to my house." My voice sounded calm to me.

"The reporter left his contact info, to see about an interview." She handed me the note, which I took with thanks. I had just declared that we saw each other regularly and I was his contact with the rest of city, but I felt fine.

She smiled, and I felt more camaraderie than teasing in it. First bridge crossed, successfully. Apparently these things didn't bother her. She was young and had other people in her to life to think about, more important than me. She'd gossip a little and that would be that. Daniel and I wouldn't be doing any more public presentations to keep the talk alive.

My classroom was full. Even the perennial absentees had appeared. Had the news spread last night in a wave of telephone calls? "The professor is sleeping with Ana's ex!" If I were a student, that would draw me to the Literature class, normally so boring but now seasoned with such juicy news.

All of them smiled at me. Ana was not there. I prayed that she was okay, that she hadn't fallen into a pit of depression provoked by love gone wrong.

I realized that I was no longer the professor with the most-private private life, and this change made them happy even if some disapproved. Ana's girlfriends would be angry, but they had no way to take revenge. Others would be defending me. Someone would have said there was really no proof, and someone else that no proof was needed. Some would say Daniel wasn't Ana's property and anyway their thing had ended. The most lighthearted would assert that the professor too had a right to "get some" once in a while. They all would be enjoying themselves, because my superiority had been knocked down a peg or two.

Also, I told myself, what if Daniel's overheated words were merely a declaration of love to which I had not yet replied? Sure, I answered, like a knight's paean to his beloved in a chivalric romance. Still, that outside chance allowed me to conduct my class without feeling accused by twenty pairs of eyes whose owners were, as usual, occupied with something other than my words.

What was different was that on this occasion they were all occupied with the same thing.

"You're a hopeless paranoid," Lorena declared as she dashed from room to room. She's always cleaning up the messes that multiply throughout her house.

"Follow me," she ordered. I pursued her through an itinerary that involved a series of quick stops to put various things back where they belonged.

"Don't you think anyone in the Department of Language and Literature has anything better to do than keep track of who you're sleeping with? Since when are you so egocentric? Believe me, by now everyone's already forgotten the whole thing. Do you like the guy? Then go for it. Nothing is free, honey. You had to steal him from his girlfriend and overcome your scruples about the difference in your ages and professions, but I haven't heard you say you want to let him go. You ought to be worrying that if you keep this shit up, he'll drop you first."

My expression said that yes, this could happen. Lorena turned around and brandished a blue-bristled hairbrush she used to splash paint on her canvases. "Your self-esteem is in the basement. You think nothing good can happen to you unless you sacrifice something else. You think that if the kids in your classroom and a couple of old-timers on the edge of retirement spend ten minutes a day talking about you, that's a disaster. Why? Because you're looking for acceptance all the time, and you don't think much of yourself. Why else would you go for a Neanderthal like your ex-husband?"

I brought her up to date on Marcos's life and future plans. She crossed herself theatrically and declaimed, "God has answered my prayers. Goodbye Marcos. Just let me know when he's actually landed someplace where he can't take advantage of your insecurities any more. Because that's what it's about with you. You're insecure. You think so little of yourself, you don't believe you deserve the kid. When are you bringing him here to meet me, by the way?"

Lorena wanted to catch up with Sergio. She loves everyone, but she's quite competitive too.

"Marian, go to bed with this youngster as often as you can, which ought to be plenty. Enjoy every minute. When your boring and orderly brain demands a forecast about the future, tell it to go to hell. You hear me?"

I nodded. Lorena scrutinized my expression so as to decide whether she'd really convinced me. Then she added, "And whenever you need to hear this again, come over, because I'll be delighted to repeat it. In these hypocritical times, it's a luxury to get to tell somebody the truth. Are you coming to my exhibition? Saturday at five. And bring him. Then we'll come back here for a party. We'll take what whatever scraps are in the refrigerator and make fried rice."

"WHAT DOES LORENA PAINT?"

Daniel was taken with the idea of going to the show and meeting everyone. He must have also been sick of my reluctance to let anyone know about us. He said I was one of those people who have to dissect every good thing until they can find the slightest flaw to make it into a problem. Meanwhile, he was enjoying how good we were together and everything we did.

"We're a great couple," he said. "You pour all your troubles on my shoulders, and I shake them off so they can't overwhelm us."

"Life is plenty hard, Marian," he explained. "From the moment we wake up, life has it in for us. The electricity goes off, there's no gas for cooking, there's no milk for breakfast unless you've got dollars to buy it with. Leave the house and you see everyone catching as catch can. All day long it's about hustling and survival. And yet you think there are people out there with time to be scrutinizing what you do."

I tried to convince him my world wasn't that way, that the university and my department were their own little world where people didn't let go of things—that his ex-girlfriend was my student, that all my students were the same age as him.

"It's precisely because everything is expensive and difficult," I argued, "that gossip has become such a source of entertainment. It's free, all you need is time and a target, and there's no shortage of those. Besides, gossiping has been proven to be healthy, because it releases endorphins and provokes pleasure."

"Just like having sex and eating bananas—two more things we can do without much trouble," he replied. "Except maybe not the bananas. The price of bananas is on a European level now, so we're not even a banana republic any more. Did you ever learn about the two-year fallow cycle?"

"No, but I remember the three-year one."

"That was in feudal Europe. The two-year one was a predecessor from the time of slavery in Egypt. That's what we are, slaves. Like in Periclean Athens, when slaves were acquired through debt or war. I love you. I'm in your debt, and you're my prisoner. I'm not planning to grant you your freedom or ask you for mine. Will you kiss me in front of everybody at your friend's exhibition? Or will you act the part of the mentor of the young man whose book you presented, whom you're now exposing to a slice of the world of art?"

"Why is that so important to you?"

"I don't know. Maybe because all the time I think I don't deserve you."

"Then it must be true." And we laughed.

THE SHOW WAS PACKED. People are very fond of Lorena, and they owe her favors too. She's put up anybody who's ever needed a bed, she's lent money, clothes, and furniture to anyone who asks. She's a locomotive that lays its own track as it goes. Once she rented a place at the beach and got thrown out the first night for having nineteen people sleeping in the only bedroom there.

If Lorena needs something, she just has to say so. Gears grind into motion, and presto, the item in question appears.

The show was in one of the best galleries. The canvases were mounted for free. The buffet was a gift, the drinks were good, and plenty of press came. The catalogue was glossy and fine, the audience lively but well-behaved.

All Lorena had to do was be the painter. P.T. saw to it that she didn't have to worry about the rest, and some of the guests took charge of the kids.

Daniel and I had agreed to meet at the gallery. He asked whether he could bring Adrián and I told him yes. When they didn't appear I began to worry they had misunderstood the address.

It was the perfect occasion, just where Daniel wanted to be introduced. Full of people who would see us together. The crowd was sufficiently youthful, because Lorena loves being everyone's mother if she's even five years older than them. She wanted to meet Daniel so she could adopt him too.

"Don't describe him to me," she said. "As soon he comes in, I'll know."

Someone delivered a speech to open the event. Someone else read a commentary on Lorena's work. She said a few words, two or three attendees asked questions, and there was a big round of applause. People spread out, formed little groups to drink, eat, and talk. Lorena brought me a cell phone and told me to call him.

"He must be on his way," I said after trying his number with no answer.

"Are you sure you told him the right place?"

"Yes, but I'm starting to worry he might have misunderstood."

Lorena stood on a chair to announce that the gallery was closing but the party would move to her house. Attendees with cars arranged to ferry those they could fit, while the rest considered what means of transport to attempt.

"I can't come over," I told her. "I don't know where Daniel is and I need to copy my grades for tomorrow."

"You can call him from my place." Lorena was intent on meeting him that night.

"No thanks," I said."Don't worry. You'll meet him before long."

I went home. Nobody was there. There was one message on the answering machine. I prayed it would be him.

It was Olga, who said she wanted to see me the next day at school. She asked me to come in a half hour early to meet with her.

I looked in the mirror and decided I ought to stay dressed a while longer, in case Daniel returned, so he could see me made up and nearly elegant.

I sat down to work. It was a tedious task, copying each student's grades for homework and tests into the proper line in the grade sheet. I made *café con leche* and set up a table lamp like the ones police use for interrogations. I placed it to the left of the papers and put on music to keep myself awake. There was no need for that, because really I was waiting up for Daniel. I was neither falling asleep nor concentrating. I tried to put the proper numbers in the proper boxes anyway.

By the time he arrived, there was nothing left of the woman who attends gallery openings with aplomb.

"Marian, I just came from the gallery. It was closed." He came closer and shined the lamp on me. "God, how beautiful you always are."

"The opening ended two hours ago. Everybody went to Lorena's house."

"I know. I called there and talked to someone who told me you had left. That's why I came here."

"The plan was for us to go together," I said while trying to concentrate on students, grades, and boxes.

"Marian, do you love me very much?"

"Yes."

"If I said, let's get married right now, would you do it?"

"No. And I don't think that has much to do with love."

"I think it does. With love and our future."

"Daniel, I've been sitting here waiting for you like a little girl, working through every stage of anxiety. I made a fool of myself in front of lots of people. And we've missed a party where we would have had a good time."

"Let's go there now."

"It's late and I'm only halfway through these grades."

"Marian, we're going to live in Madrid. Happily ever after, like at the end of a story book. That's the news I'm bringing. Say yes, and then we'll go to Lorena's party, right now. When we get back, we'll talk the whole thing through."

Daniel's news shook me down to my bones. Leave Cuba? Go and leave everything behind? Start over. One less here, one more over there. Leave, just like that. Like in a magic show, climb into a box and with two shakes of the wand you disappear and emerge somewhere else. In Madrid. Happy and dining on roast quail and rioja.

I dropped everything on the table as an avalanche of angry words began to pour out. We had never talked about such a thing. I had no idea Daniel was harboring an intention to leave. Or that he would need to confirm this plan right now, after standing me up and keeping me waiting for hours, worried and longing for him to appear.

"What are you going to do when you get to Madrid? Wash floors? Drill concrete with an air hammer in front of the Puerta de Alcalá? Or do you think the city is full of rich older women who are waiting to put a bank account in your name and take you to pick out the car you want to drive?"

I could have gone on and on, each detail crueler than the one before. Something had blown open and I didn't want to stop the torrent.

"I'm going to do whatever I can, while I write and find a way to publish. I'm going to live and dream that one day I'll do more. Spain is full of publishers. I'll be a writer there."

"Sure, the editors at Planeta are waiting to give you a prize and a fat advance. Do you really think it's that easy?"

"Yes, I do. I'll work like a slave, wear myself out doing whatever I find, enough to live a decent life. When I come home from whatever shitty job I have at the beginning, that home will be a tiny, cold, unfurnished room, but it will be mine. I'll sit down to write—also like a slave—until I've got something really good. Then I'll pound the pavement for hours and cool my heels for centuries and lick the butts of editors and their secretaries and finally I'll publish, or win a contest, and I won't let any opportunity pass me by. And then, that's when you'll come."

"I'm not interested in being the wife of an immigrant, waiting for him to make his way in the First World so I can go there and live as a foreigner whom everyone despises."

"I thought you loved me."

"I thought the same, but you've made very definite plans without consulting me. And now guess what? I don't want to share them."

"Then come with me right away. We won't have anything at first, but we can still spend Sunday afternoons on the lawns of the Retiro, or go to museums that have free admission on weekends. Every Sunday, a new painting in the Prado! Can you picture that?"

"No. What I can picture is that we won't be able to pay the rent, and with luck we'll end up on someone's couch, and they'll give us seventy-two hours to find someplace else. During those seventy-two hours we'll use the daylight hours to fall into despair and the nighttime ones to wonder why we came."

"Who's been telling you horror stories like that?"

"Who's been telling you fairy tales? Madrid is cold and hard."

"So we'll go farther south. Everything is easier and cheaper. You can teach classes in some kind of school, and I'll do whatever it takes. I'm young. It's now or never, Marian."

I took his hands as if I could make him see reason.

"I love you, Daniel, and don't want to live without you. But I like living here and I don't want to leave. Over there I'm not going to have a housel like this one. I won't be a professor in a university. I won't know where I am or who I am. The other things don't interest me. I don't think they're so important. I don't want to be the last card in an unknown deck in a game I've never played before."

"You already are the last card in the deck. Poorer than any waiter, taxi driver, or cashier in a dollar store. What life have you got? A useless car rotting in the garage because you can't get it fixed. A house that empties out little by little as you turn possessions into money. Money you have to save for the day you don't have anything left to sell. When was the last time you gave yourself a treat? Went out for dinner, bought yourself a dress? You're not wise in the ways of the world, Marian. You could sell the car on the black market, rent out rooms, organize yourself some trips abroad through your department. But you don't know how to do any of that. And eventually it'll all come home to roost. I'm telling you that I'll go to work for you until I can offer you something better. We'll have a good life. You'll be a teacher, not a waitress, and one night we'll find ourselves in the Alhambra watching our reflections in the fountain we read about in Washington Irving. We'll take vacations in Istanbul and Tangier. Do you know there are flights to Paris and Rome for pennies, on airlines based in Ireland?"

"Where did you hear all this?"

I was no longer being intolerant. I was just trying to play for time, to find out what kernel of truth lay at the bottom of these crazy plans. Something must have happened to provoke all this.

"Go to bed. I'll finish copying the grades, you're exhausted. I have to take care of you. Go on."

We made love. Daniel, as if he couldn't live without me in Spain or anywhere else on earth. I, as if to remind him that our world here was good and safe. He, thinking I'd go with him. I, that he wouldn't go anywhere. Nobody copied anything onto the grade sheets. Nobody went to sleep. It was as if we had to use every minute. As if, when we closed our eyes, the other would be gone.

We said over and over that our only country was the time and space in which we were together. But not even that mattered.

79

We were in a bed of snow-white clouds, and everything around us disappeared with an abracadabra we chanted in unison when we started to make love.

I WAS LATE GETTING to work. Olga had gone off to a meeting, but she left a note on my desk. She said we'd have to talk another day.

Meanwhile, things did not go very well. I was behind on various tasks. Three students wanted me to recheck their exams. The two who had missed the test wanted me to substitute a research paper the way I had for Ana. Daniel didn't call. I claimed to have a headache, which ended up being true, so I gave the students the afternoon off. That was the only positive moment of my workday, when the relief that flooded their faces made me feel like a generous soul.

When I got home, I went right to the answering machine. Four messages, none from Daniel. But three from Spanish women who were trying to find him. Two different voices, ages unclear. Messages laced with humor, suggesting a degree of intimacy.

I took a shower, and then a sedative. I sat down to work, to catch up. The way I used to do, when there was no Daniel and I lived peacefully and worked well. When I was a well-respected professor. Et cetera. I kept winding the spring tighter. I went over the exams the students had asked me to review, and decided not to give an inch on the grades. I invented research tasks for the opportunists making use of Ana to avoid taking the test. I made sure they would spend enough time searching out books, reading them, taking notes and processing them into a written paper that they would regret having chosen this alternative.

I worked all afternoon. Tomorrow I'd arrive at the university with all my papers in order, just as I used to, I said, which made me feel better about myself. I'd be my own ally in coping with whatever was coming next.

None of this changed what happened when he showed up. Something inside me relaxed and let me embrace him more docilely than I had planned. I consoled myself with the thought that this was a wiser strategy than confronting him head on.

"We're bedding down on the floor," he said. "Get the cushions, let's open the door to the porch, and I'll make us whipped lemonade with crushed ice. Okay? It's so hot."

"Let's," I said, and began straightening up the porch. This is such a beautiful view, I thought, arranging the cushions and gazing out at the sea. I don't know how anyone can imagine going anywhere else.

When Daniel was settled in beside me, I said, "There's a guy who wants to buy the car. He'll give me ten thousand dollars, because he's got a way of registering it under his name. We'll be able to get by for a quite a while on that. You can sit down to write without worrying about money. How much have they offered you in Madrid?"

I could have skipped the last question. I thought I was putting him on notice, but what came out of his mouth was nothing like what I expected.

"The next book is what I want to talk about. My idea is for us to write it together. But first I want us to make love right here, right now, with the doors open. If anyone's looking, all they'll see are two little bodies. And if that someone has the patience to study us through a pair of binoculars, let's give them the show they deserve. Or should we talk about the book first? We can leave the car for later."

I didn't want to make love or talk about the book. Nor was I a writer, I thought. I was a professor, and a good one, and I'd neglected that for him. I'd just gotten reorganized and wanted to stay that way. And I wanted to know how he was organizing himself. There was a lot that needed clearing up.

It was hard to reconcile these desires for clarity and serious conversation, however, with the calm sea, cloudless sky, and afternoon heat that only increased the attractions of lounging on the floor and drinking frozen lemonade out of a frosted glass. I would have preferred to have never heard those messages on the machine, and for there to be no Iberian Peninsula looming between us and darkening the day. Still, I returned to the attack.

"Were the voices speaking Old World Spanish into my answering machine the same ones that told you about the beauties of Madrid?"

"Did they call? Ohmygod, I told them they'd get to meet you today. We agreed they'd take us out to eat, someplace that you and I would choose. How could I forget? I was home all day, writing, and my phone is cut off because I didn't pay the bill. That's why I couldn't call you at work. The nearest pay phone is half a mile away. I asked the nurse downstairs to call you from the hospital when she got there, but probably she couldn't, or she forgot. I'm exhausted, but I've got so many things to tell you. Look, I've got the outline all done. We'll do it together. We don't need a style in common, we're two voices, each telling the story our way, and each can be the judge of the other. It's better than having a kid. Have you thought that we might have a kid? We haven't taken any precautions."

And he laughed, happy with that sudden realization. He had forgotten all about the women who'd called. As if they really didn't matter to him.

So maybe he'd forgotten about his desire to leave as well. Maybe the fever had peaked and passed. He wanted to write, and where could he do that better than here? Maybe he had figured that out, I thought, observing his boyish pleasure.

"They're high school teachers from Alcalá de Henares. They want to meet you. And yes, they are the ones who were telling me about Madrid and its advantages, the bookstores and contests and publishers and the pleasures of travel. But they haven't offered me anything, and I haven't asked. I thought we could take advantage of the dinner, and bring it up then."

The plans we'd each made. The clarity I wanted from him. The late afternoon sunlight. How tired I felt. How vital he seemed. I watched him as I counted all these factors up.

"I'm tired, Daniel. I really am. I've had a bad day, I was miles behind on everything, and I've just caught up. Here's what we'll do. You call them, and you go out. Tell them I'm not feeling well, that I'll meet them another time. Tell them you'd love to go to Alcalá and see the house where Cervantes was born. Bring two copies of your book, sign one for each, and bring a third for them to circulate and see what they can do. Tell me all about it when you come back. I'll wait up for you."

"No way," he said. "We won't go, that's all. You lie down and get a little sleep while I make dinner. Then we'll sit on the porch and talk about the book."

"Does it have a title?"

"It'll be called *Bonjour Tristesse*."

"Does Françoise Sagan know that?"

"Can't we use the same title in a different language?"

"I don't think so."

"Are you going to tell me there are no books with the same title anywhere in the world?"

"I don't know."

"Well, sleep on it, and I'll cook on it, and then we'll report. Now go on, to bed with you."

"No. I want to make love. I'm very happy right now."

"So am I, Marian."

I didn't go to sleep, and Daniel didn't make dinner. By ten at night the breeze was blowing in from all sides and we were making a potato omelet and toast, and deciding whether to blow the milk supply on a mango shake, or save it and juice the mango with water.

"We'll write vignettes. About the city. The real one, the one you don't see in calendars or postcards. The everyday one, with its small poverties. It's important to tell small details. Like those photos in which everyday details reveal so much. I'll include mine and you'll include yours. Short scenes, narrated with a certain detachment."

I listened to these instructions. I wondered whether I could do that. At least I could try.

The phone rang while my hands were drenched in mango. Daniel picked it up. Them, of course, the witches of Alcalá. Not letting go of their prey. I washed my hands and left the omelet to burn in the pan and the bread in the oven. I didn't want to hear this conversation. I sat down on the porch. *Bonjour Tristesse*.

Since I met him, I haven't had a moment of peace, I up-braided myself. I never know whether or not he's telling the truth, and then I feel bad for having thought the worst of him. I'm torn between stratagems that aren't like me and remorse over being distrustful. And then in the end he does what he wants and I enjoy it.

The conversation dragged on. I tried not to hear Daniel's voice, which was sounding very smooth.

That's the problem, I thought, while every minute of waiting turned into a century. When things are going well, I feel so happy that I'll do anything to keep them going well. Including sending him off to have dinner with those two.

"Marian, there's a fellowship in Alcalá for writers from abroad, younger than twenty-five, with only one book published. They've filled out the application for me already. They know people in the embassy. Their school has contacts with small publishers who can take on my book. I can give lectures. The fellowship starts in two months. The Writers Union here will help me with the red tape. They've already been to the Union to talk about it. Marian, they're terrific. You see? We're in luck."

He wasn't shouting. The news didn't surprise or rattle him. He knelt down and laid his head on my thighs and so, caressing me, whispered the good news.

The streetlights along the Malecón had gone off. Out in the dark sea, there was just one luminous thread. The cruise ship full of foreigners marveling at the city, perhaps.

WHEN MY CLASSES ENDED I met with Olga, who was waiting for me but made no mention of our previous missed appointment.

"How would you like to be department head for a while?" she asked.

She smiled at my surprise. She reminded me of Ray Bradbury's "Illustrated Woman." Was the map of my destiny tattooed somewhere underneath her rainbow fabrics? Did everything that happened to me start with some proposition of hers? Was my response to her questions the famous fork in the road where we make our crucial decisions?

I had no Cheshire Cat to ask which path to take. I had to decide all alone and later regret or congratulate myself.

Amidst these thoughts, I kept my eyes on Olga, who, in keeping with the professional vice of all teachers, set about explaining how the department works. Teaching tasks, administrative ones, political ones. Not forgetting the gossip and legends of the locale.

Olga told me all the marvels of the kingdom she was abandoning in order to go the University of Iceland as a part of a collaboration with the Classical Languages department there. She spread files and documents before me like a ship's captain demonstrating his vessel's course to a sailor. In her telling, it was all attractive and intellectually absorbing.

But, at the same time, it was a big responsibility. It wasn't enough to be intelligent and dedicated. It required, too, craftiness and a certain dose of underhandedness. Fighting a ton of people inclined to pull the wool over your eyes so as to work as little as possible. Being the court of last resort for many quarrels among both students and professors. And then there were the inspections by outside authorities. Academic, trade union, political, economic. Some of them worthy of the Inquisition.

Finally, the skills of diplomacy. To maintain harmonious relations with an endless list of powerful and influential people to whom you might have to turn, at any moment, for help in solving problems, or avoiding them. Or so that these eminences would bathe the department in their talents and beneficence, so we too could reach certain destinations—or, at least, stay afloat.

"The secretary has background and contacts for all these people in her book, but you also have to have them at hand yourself, because they're very useful, and whenever you travel you need to be sure to bring that information with you."

Travel, the golden apple of our unending national desire. Most of Olga's trips are to Spain, home of the Royal Academy, the great publishing houses, the linguists with pedigrees. Home of Madrid, the city of Daniel's writerly dreams. Something inside me ignited then, sparked by those same dreams.

Olga listed the necessary emails and telephone numbers. The Spanish Embassy, the Spanish Cultural Center, the Ibero-American Center. The consul, the cultural attaché. University professors, writers, editors, poets, essayists, and journalists. All woven together, amidst their spatial ebbs and flows, in the web of a linguistic world stretching from the most forgotten corner of Old Castile to the most forgotten corner of the most forgotten country in Latin America.

I told her I'd think it over, and I said goodbye to her Van Gogh sunflower smile. From the hallway I looked back at the closed door and its legend, "Spanish language department," as if it were a tree in which the Cat might appear. I recalled that another offer of Olga's had placed *The Eskimo* in my purse and Daniel in my life.

I went down the stairs as the last class of the day was letting out. I had traded my habitual slow pace for the rapid, anxious steps and attention to the clock of someone hurrying to a party. It's true that something changes in the eyes of people in love. But we always think that such love is the stuff of soap operas and bad novels.

Seated on a bench in the entranceway was Daniel. He smiled and stood with open arms.

Behind me, I could hear my students, the bustle of happy

young people released from class. In between them and Daniel, me—and my expression of a cheerful idiot, embarrassed by the number of witnesses.

"Have you been waiting long?"

"No. I spent the whole day with the Spanish women, working. They interviewed me for their school magazine and for an educational channel. They paid me. We've got money and we're going out to spend it right now."

"We don't need to. Let's go home and you can tell me there."

"Let's go out someplace nice, and I'll tell you there. Hi, Ana."

There she stood, looking as pleased as if she'd orchestrated our encounter herself. They kissed affectionately, like old friends who once went to bed together because they were bored.

"Are you doing okay, Daniel?" asked Ana with a generous smile.

"If Marian loves me, yes."

"So you'd better find out," she answered with a shake of her golden locks. The she was off with the strides of a young girl to whom everything has been promised and everything is permitted.

We took a taxi that charged in dollars, which is to say it had comfortable seats, no sweaty passengers, and a friendly and conversational driver of the sort that figures everything out right away. Daniel told him to drive along the Malecón, take the tunnel under the bay, and deliver us to the Divina Pastora restaurant on the other side. And to wait for us there.

"Why such drastic expense?" I asked. "Did you get paid for a couple of interviews, or did you rob a bank or collect for some other dirty deed?"

The restaurant sits on an outdoor patio whose walls are the old stones of a Spanish fortress. Below us, the bay and a sunset which began to tint the calm water and the buildings of the city on the other side. Daniel asked for the wine list, chose a rioja, and suggested entrees for me to order, smiling a sweet and mischievous smile. Watching him take charge, navigate this atmosphere that would be ours for only a few hours, I felt in the presence of a skillful young emperor. I managed to forget about everything and my eyes teared up. I never know how to deal with too many good things at once.

"I haven't told you about my father, how much I owe him. It's thanks to him I'm a survivor. When I was a kid he taught me to walk through the whole house in the dark, without a sound."

"Like an Indian," I said.

We finished eating. Daniel asked for the bill, paid it including an appropriate tip, and back we went to our waiting taxi. As we emerged from the tunnel on the city side, he asked the driver to stop and let us out.

"Let's walk a while before going home. Then I'll finish telling you about my father. The next part isn't so pretty."

As is so often the case, the Malecón offered the only breeze in the city. The sky went from pink to red, purple, and a light blue that darkened as the streetlights came on, like a theater as the show is about to begin.

Darkness fell, a work of both God and the defects of the electricity department. We sat on the seawall. The lights that should have illuminated this section of the drive were off. It's quite rare to see the Malecón lit from one end to the other.

"Yet we know it's there," he said. "And we know that beyond is the *mare nostrum* that encloses the city. You can smell it, can't you?"

He put his head between my legs and started to talk, whispering into those other lips. He told them about the Tartars who marched onward impelled by a thirst for battle and victory, while inside me everything grew damp with that warlike and bloody epic. From the center of the angle formed by my wide-open legs, Daniel sensed my excitement, savoring every second and every inch, and then he described exactly what was happening to me. I felt that everything trembling within me was responding to the order encased in his words.

"My father begat me in a few moments of pleasure—my mother was quite a beauty, I already told you that. Then he spent years trying to destroy me, trying to show me I was no good for anything in life. Now he lives in Las Vegas, the ideal place for him, where he's waiting confidently for news of failures and humiliations to trickle in one at a time. I think he'd rather have that than win thousands at the slot machines or poker tables."

We were home now, in my house which seemed to be another piece of this night full of mirages. We turned off all the lights. The moon, round and full of gossip, drank in our confessions.

"To show me that I was no man, no heterosexual stud who could handle a woman in bed, he offered me his girlfriend—one of many who came to the strange parties in my house, where there was lots of drinking and then everyone ended up in the sack. She was my first woman. I was fourteen and she was twenty-two. Our relationship lasted a few weeks. When my father was at work, she'd come over, I'd skip school, and we'd spend the day together. One night I got home late and found the usual party. My father's bedroom door was closed, and so was the door to the bathroom. Since I wanted to use the bathroom, I knocked. My father opened, drunk out of his mind. With an evil look, he led me in to where I could see his "friend," whom I thought of as my girlfriend, making love with another girl. The world spun, my head wanted to explode, and everything went blurry. I ran out of the house, to the funeral parlor, and slept there, slumped in an armchair.

"To show me I'd never be a writer, he took me to meet a real one. That man read my stuff and liked it. He told me to keep writing. At his house is where I met Adrián.

"So I owe my father a lot of things. The opinion of a writer who encouraged me to keep going, the chance to meet my best friend, and the certainty that sex is something too wonderful to be subject to any rules."

"And that woman?"

"She's fine. She's a photographer. She was already a very good photographer when we met. She broke off contact with my father, but she's always stayed in touch with me."

We made love. I wanted to protect Daniel from his father, from the horror of his adolescent first love. From adversity and from his own bad ideas. I wanted him to stay inside me and become my lover and my child. I wanted to be everything for him— his mother, his planet, his fate.

"It seems we all want to take care of you, Daniel. First that woman, then me, and now the teachers from Alcalá," I said, kissing his shoulder.

"They're not teachers," he told me then. He took both my hands as if compelling me to listen. "They're just a pair of tourists who want to enjoy themselves every way they can—and they know they have pay for such things. I never went to the gallery. I called Lorena's house from my place, where the two of them were with me. I was disgusted and needed to hear your voice. You're the best thing that's ever happened to me. That night, looking at the two of them, so drunk and so ordinary, I needed you very much. I thought of you, shy and frightened, trying to live a decent life, trying to stay untainted by the shit that drenches us day by day. It's hard, Marian, but you keep trying."

I wanted to shush him, yet his story drew me like iron to a magnet. Through my fear, I tried to marshal my courage so as to say something.

"I watched them, naked, laughing like geese, ugly, indecent. I thought, 'They've got passports, they can go wherever they please, they have houses, cars, jobs. They go out and drink in bars, have dinner with friends, celebrate Christmas, buy things, make plans. When they're old, they'll have lived plenty.' It seemed unfair that we couldn't do the same. And almost cruel that you don't even want to, that you don't dream, that you don't realize what we deserve. All the marvels that they talk about were made for us. You deserve a birthday where I can give you nice presents and take you out to eat or we can take a trip to a romantic village, one of the many out there waiting for us."

So much loomed over me: airplanes, Velázquez's paintings, Toledo and the Alhambra, clubbing in Madrid, European high culture—that whole other life.

Without being aware, I'd curled up in the chair, into the classic fetal position of the helpless and depressed. Daniel seemed large and dark, fearfully secure in the night and his confessions.

"So go to Madrid," I managed to say, "and become a great writer and then I'll come join you and teach in a school and we'll have a little house for just the two of us and nights of wine and Sunday strolls. And Coca-Cola all the time. Do you know who Claudio Abbado is?"

"Not the slightest idea."

"One of the greatest orchestra conductors in the world. He's appeared here a number of times. The last one, I went and saw him. The ticket cost me less than half a dollar. The orchestra played Mozart, Beethoven, and Mahler for a price equivalent to twenty-five cents. Like the theater and the ballet. But to buy a Coke at intermission costs a full dollar. I can hear music exquisitely performed and see good plays for pennies, but to poison myself with chilled caffeine costs me an arm and a leg. I don't know that I want to trade. To have Coca-Cola in the refrigerator and drink it every night so as to forget that I'm an undocumented dishwasher in a foreign city and to exorcise the exhaustion and the doubt that it's all worthwhile?"

"That's all you expect out of life. A concert every Sunday afternoon. There's no way to get to the theater, the taxi costs more than the show, and on the way out you're wondering whether you'll find a way to get home. No sitting down over coffee and discussing whether or not you liked the show. You can't be serious! How can anybody say they'd prefer to listen to music without knowing what they'll have for breakfast the next day, or how they'll get to work—and with knowing that every day will be like that, and knowing that anyone who can, leaves, and those who stay behind are exactly the ones who can live the way you don't know how to, those who live by their wits, who chant socialist slogans today and tomorrow are out stealing whatever they can. And for a sound track, Mozart melodies for half a dollar. Are you crazy?"

"It doesn't seem crazy to want to live in my country. Or there must be a lot of crazy people around. Or is it that I belong to a group you left out of your list? The group for whom being here is more important than the superlatives of over there. People who work and complain and protest because they think everything should be better. Who want everything to be better, just like other people in other places do. Maybe they're the most ambitious group of all. I want there to be buses, *café con leche*, and concerts, but I want them here. I want to be here, Daniel, and I want you with me. I want you to have time to write and real reasons to do it well. Do you see? I want some things too."

"No. You don't want anything. You don't want to be famous, or rich, or healthy, or happy."

"And you want too many things at once. Your first novel will be all about how awful things are here—or maybe your first three. Airing all our dirty laundry, and I'm sure they'll be magnificent, because you'll have plenty of material to draw on. But then you'll run out of plots because you'll no longer know what's going on here, and then what you'll write will be junk. Which won't matter, as long as it's got bad things, sad things, or violent ones. Until the publishers get tired of the same and more of the same, when they'll trade you in for another young writer just off the plane, who's brought newer, fresher, and smellier shit, because yours no long stinks enough."

"Sure, because the only literature being written in the world is the kind that trashes Cuba. Of course. Saramago's novels all begin on the Malecón. Paul Auster's are about tourists in Havana and the girls they pick up. Tabucchi, Pamuk. . . . Who said *we* were so important? Real literature isn't denouncing Cuba and socialism for three hundred pages seasoned with sex and local color. The world is full of stories, which writers see in their own ways. And they tell them, and when they tell them well, they win. I'm not talking about scribbling, I'm talking about writing. Telling. There's life everywhere, Marian. I'm going to write. I'm going to win. And I'll keep asking you the same question—do you want to marry me, Marian?—from over there.

"Why?"

"I told you why, because I love you. And when all the good things that are coming arrive, I want to be with you."

"No, why did you decide to tell me the truth?"

"Because you deserve it. Because you're able to understand that the reason I've told you so many lies is to accomplish something for the two of us. I told the Spaniards that a Frenchwoman wants to take me to Paris, so they'll feel they've got competition. They said that Paris sucks, that it rains all the time and the French are insufferable.

"And why should I believe this is the truth?"

"Because you're smart and you know I love you and that my plans with you are real. That's my truth."

"I'm afraid it's not enough. We're many years removed from the Romantic Age."

"I never thought I'd hear you say that love isn't enough. It's what we can pit against war, evil, greed, infidelity, and envy. It helps us believe in ourselves and in others, in something better for everyone. In a better world. But for you it's just a literary period. You're small-minded and cerebral. You don't have dreams, or brainstorms either. You don't have anything. Stay here among your piles of old junk and your dead writers of the past. Masturbate remembering how I've loved every inch of you and what I would have done to keep you: tell lies, ask for favors, pay for them in bed, even deny you exist. All so that one day I could arrive in a new and different place, work, be someone, and finally lay it all in front of you and say, 'Come be with me.' You're a pile of shit. I hope you rot in the hell of those who have never sinned. You're disgustingly sterile. I'm going, Marian."

He stood there before me, I thought, like an accused man awaiting a verdict. Or an actor awaiting applause.

"Go Daniel, and slam the door the way you do every time something happens that you don't like: what I think about your book, or about us, or about the country. Slam the door to my house, to the airport, to the plane. I'll masturbate remembering that you're ready to do anything for me except stay with me."

There was a silence that stretched for centuries. Daniel walked slowly, as if I were asleep and he had to be careful not to wake me. He closed the door very softly, as if kissing my forehead or taking my hand.

The mechanic poked his head out from under the car to sing me the well-known song that it was a wreck and whoever was buying it was acquiring a problem.

I had decided to sell it, and who better than a mechanic to find me a buyer? They know everyone who's in the market for a used automobile—people with the money, the desire, and no earthly way to get authorization to buy one new.

So I also sang him my well-known song, that selling the car was no big deal to me, that I wasn't going to lose any sleep over whether it happened or not. I adopted the air of someone trying to shake off an object she really didn't want to have around anymore, for whom economic need was a strictly secondary aspect.

The third act of this opera involved each of us trying to avoid falling into the trap of the other. So we came to a face-off in the neutral territory where there were no great obstacles to selling the car, and I was getting rid of it because I'd rather have the money than a Moskvich that made such exhausting demands.

"Do you want it fixed before you sell it, or would you rather get rid of it right away?"

Now the lyrics were growing more difficult. They required a mix of Muscovite auto mechanics and Swiss bank calculus. We grappled a bit and decided on rendering the car as attractive as possible with a minimum of expense. He told me he didn't want any percentage of the sale, which implied that his profit was already built into the price of the absolutely necessary repairs, which meant that the minimum would be far from minimal. That's how these things usually go.

The mechanic managed to get the Moskvich started and drove it up the ramp from the garage. He waved happily and took off into the distance as if the car had never belonged to me.

I said to myself, aloud, "Goodbye car." I didn't feel anything, other than a temptation to call Daniel to tell him about it. As if selling the car, something that for us here is a very serious operation with grave consequences, was important only in offering me a reason to get in touch with him.

Or try to get in touch. Because in fact I had already called him quite a few times since he had left my house.

At first I was afraid of giving myself away. As if the mere ring of the telephone would finger me as the caller, rather as I'd feel if discovered in act of picking someone's pocket. However, caller ID is a very scarce service here, a completely unnecessary luxury, so one's anonymity is almost always guaranteed. One of the advantages of underdevelopment: mystery.

Daniel had no answering machine. These too are not very abundant. Even if he did, I wouldn't have been able to leave him a message, because then I'd have cast myself in the role of waiting for him to call me back.

So I was thankful that Daniel had no answering machine and that I could call him without giving myself away.

The first few times I hung up on the second ring. Later, more bravely, I let it ring longer, secure in being just one more caller.

The last few times, I let it keep ringing until the line automatically went dead. I sat there, listening to one ring-ring after another, while my heart beat with the hope that this monotonous and familiar sound would be interrupted by a voice. After a while I calmed down and just listened peacefully, convinced that this sound, which told me he wasn't home, also contained some kind of sympathy for me.

I thought of using the most common ploy, most frequently in

use among teenagers: that I wanted to "give him back his things." But Daniel hadn't left anything at my house. I didn't realize that until I needed something return to him, and came up empty.

Or maybe not. There was *The Arabian Nights*.

Before taking it to him, I washed my hair and chose my outfit. I put myself together carefully, as if getting ready for a date. All to play a single card, which would get him to open a door and take the book, maybe thanking me and maybe not. Or maybe that would lead to something more.

I found his house, an apartment building from the 1930s that he had called "pure Havana art deco." Through the grime, yes, the style could still be glimpsed. I knew he lived on the top floor. The stairway was more comfortable and better lit than I expected.

I knocked, praying that he'd be slow enough to give my expression of fear and anxiety a chance to slip away.

Nobody came. Having foreseen this possibility, I sat down on the steps. Having exams to grade, I spread out my professorial apparatus like one building barricades and digging trenches. Since it was the top floor, I wouldn't be getting in anybody's way. And I would be so lost in my task that his arrival would truly surprise me.

I couldn't concentrate. Every sound of footsteps might be Daniel. People came in constantly. I counted the steps to keep track of which floor they reached, and each time someone kept climbing, the real possibility drove off my fright, leaving only anxiety and a desire to see him.

I remember him telling me that, although he lived alone, the apartment belonged to his grandmother. She hated him, and so as not to have deal with him, she spent almost all her time in the country at the house of a cousin whom Daniel had barely ever met but who spoiled the grandmother with the clear goal of inheriting her apartment when she died. The tactics of this distant cousin had been successful, the grandmother having made out a will in his favor. The cousin had already told the old lady that he would

be moving in and fixing up the house, which implied dire consequences for Daniel's abode and his freedom.

But neither of these relatives seemed to have taken possession
of the apartment yet. Maybe it was all just another of Daniel's
stories, I thought, smiling without bitterness. I missed Daniel and
his lies, and I'd come there in search of them.

Two hours later, I decided to station myself in the park across
the street. An awful place, laid out atop the ruins of a building
which, in the seventies, must have been architecturally sumptuous
and economically vital. It had housed the Council of Mutual Economic Assistance, an organization through which socialist countries provided each other with disinterested help, favoring the less
developed like ourselves.

As a premonition, the construction began to show signs of
trouble from the bottom up. The foundation was not well designed. The subsoil was not appropriate, so the plan for a magnificent pseudo-Corbusier edifice many stories high devolved into
a gray and prefabricated cube of four stories, pockmarked with
holes that never succeeded in looking like windows.

And later, not even that remained. The building was demol-
ished, leaving behind an enormous empty lot, a plain on which to
taste and swallow the dust of defeat.

The solution, eventually, was a park. Treeless, in a city
where the sun is an almost punitive presence. With gray bench-
es, poorly cast and scattered and isolated from each other, lampposts laid out in military style, and some sad shrubs, always
recently planted, flanking a cement-tile walkway. As if the park
had been constructed not only on top of, but out of the ruins
of the headquarters of those Magi who had come, as usual,
from the East.

The rest of the park was dry ground above which circulated
the fumes from buses and cars passing on the avenues that framed
it. These too were filled with dirty, severe gray buildings.

It was a sad redoubt, but it gave me a good view of the

entranceway to Daniel's building. I stopped grading tests so as not to let my eyes wander from the door.

Meanwhile I tried to picture what Daniel's place must look like inside. I constructed my image out of what he had told me. I had no idea how much of that was real.

According to him, the apartment was devoid of any and all of the electrical appliances that are inevitable in modern domestic life. Just an electric fan, christened "Hurricane" for the strength of its beneficent breeze. Made from the motor of a Russian washing machine. Also, a black-and-white television that functioned only if you gave it the right sort of kick. Daniel called it "Justine" and said that, since he didn't like mistreating it, he rarely turned it on.

"The best thing is about my house is, the power never goes out." So he told me one day while we were gazing over the darkened city from my porch. "Blackouts just make me laugh. The good neighborhoods and the houses with VCRs, PlayStations, DVDs, cordless phones, and microwaves go without power. Meanwhile, I've got plenty of kilowatts and no appliances the invest them in."

According to Daniel, the walls of his apartment were colored somewhere between green and gray, and the ceiling had been white many years before. The windows were beige, with French louvered panes grown dusty and squeaky and not closing very well. In the bathroom, the constant flow of water that couldn't be shut off had worn away the enamel of sink, tub, and toilet. The bathroom opened into two bedrooms furnished with old frames, battered mattresses, and very used sheets.

The floors were of gray tiles. Dull, scratched, and very seldom cleaned. In spite of the rooms being small, the lack of furniture made them feel bare.

The kitchen was tiny, everything in it proclaiming the flight of both food and inhabitants. The counter was broken, and the sink dripped. The 1950s Westinghouse refrigerator was almost always empty and in need of defrosting.

The only luxury was the computer, a present from Adrián. Though not the most modern, it was fine for writing on.

I placed Daniel in every room. Curiously, I didn't imagine anyone else with him. There was no need. It hurt me enough to imagine him carrying out innocent activities without me. I was jealous of the rusted surface of the bathroom mirror, of the back of the chair on which he tossed his jumbled clothes. Jealous of the space and time in which he moved. Jealous that he hadn't left me for another woman, but rather for himself.

I watched the people walking by. For mid-morning on a workday, there were many. Under an intensely bright blue sky, they performed a sort of choreography of idleness. People in no hurry to get anywhere, proponents of the here and now.

When the sun got too hot to bear, I couldn't lie in wait any more. With *The Arabian Nights* still in my bag, I joined the slow-moving crowd. I wished I could have been that peddler, pedaling my way home.

MY ANSWERING MACHINE WAS no longer just an appliance. It had become an ally whom I placed in charge of Daniel's re-appearance, so that I would not be condemned to wait anxiously in the house.

Sometimes I wandered aimlessly, dawdling more than I planned, confiding in the machine to reach an understanding with Daniel, as if it were a complicit mother who knew how to manage such matters for her daughter's benefit. Sometimes, while I went walking to delay my return home, I would have an attack of sudden joy because I knew the answering machine was there, watching over my relationship, ready to take the call I expected any minute.

When I did come home, I would restrain myself from rushing to the bedroom corner that my imagination had converted to the apse of a cathedral, the space that held the black box full of messages that always included Daniel's.

Instead, quelling my hurry, I would turn toward the bathroom, because the first thing one does on coming in from the street is to wash one's hands and face. I would look at myself in the mirror and confirm that, in those minutes "before," my face took on a very peculiar expression.

Then I would walk to to the kitchen and drink some water, as one also does on coming home after so much sun on the street and so few beverages available to slake one's thirst. I would not be able to avoid wondering what I'd make for dinner if Daniel were coming that night.

Sometimes I even managed to get myself out on the balcony to take a look at the city Daniel wanted to leave, with which I had signed a nonaggression pact and a tacit understanding too.

But normally, after my glass of water and the fantasy of a supper for two, I went to my corner and pressed the button. Always with cold hands and shaky legs.

The few moments that followed, those voices speaking in series, became the compass needle of my days, the indicator of my emotional state. Lorena's energetic calls ceased to have any importance, as did P.T.'s calm and collected voice, Sergio's sweetness, calls from the department to inform me of meetings or schedules, and Marcos's announcement of his departure for London that very night.

This last one, I thought with some irony, meant that Marcos had decided that my having a new lover was not sufficient reason for him to leave without calling, but it did excuse him from paying a farewell visit. I didn't stop to think about the years we'd shared or how different our lives would be from now on. Even within the limited square kilometers of our city and island, they were already different enough. What I did feel was that his message usurped the space of the other man whom I needed. And that Marcos, as usual, went about his business and accomplished what he wanted, while I was the loser he expected me to be. I went on listening to messages, always awaiting the next.

After these sessions of listening, I would cry—sometimes sadly and serenely, sometime with anger not yet used up. Sometimes, out of pure desperation, I nearly screamed.

To try to live at peace with myself, to avoid feeling guilty of having let the best thing in my life slip away, I moved on from guilt to seeing myself as the victim of a bad throw of fate's dice. I felt very sorry for myself then.

But at other times, I played tricks. I told myself Daniel had called but didn't want to talk to the answering machine. So I spent the rest of the day expectantly, imagining him behind every click when some caller, on hearing the recorded greeting, hung up without a word.

At night I would hug the pillow fiercely and try to forget I had a body. I didn't want to remember what it had experienced, but I remembered nonetheless. I refused to pay it solitary homage, which would be too painful. I cried a lot, slept badly. I considered sleeping pills, wine, infusions, good movies, and bad books, all of which can put one to sleep.

IN THE DAYS FOLLOWING the breakup, my friends paraded through my house. But nobody could help me evoke him. They didn't know him, and I had no memories to share with them. I cried in Sergio's arms, cried with P.T. holding my hand, cried with Lorena looking me straight in the face. I became a pathetic character from a soap opera, jilted episode after episode, the crybaby of the series. I told myself the same things time and time again, and wondered whether I should wait for him.

Lorena told me what she thought. "Since you don't have anything better to do, you might as well wait for him. You're going to wait for him no matter what, and how long that lasts depends on how long you delay meeting someone else, given that you're the type who clings to the past." That observation referred to Marcos, whom Lorena could never let pass an opportunity to mention. "I'm sure you'll weave and unweave the same shroud for quite a while."

I'm not going to a psychologist to talk about being "lovesick," I said to myself one day, when I was giving myself a series of orders before undertaking another twenty-four hours of waiting.

I'm not going to end up at a psychiatrist with manic-depressive bipolar disorder, I went on.

I'm not going to take sleeping pills, anti-anxiety pills, or antidepressants.

I'm not joining the cult of herbs, aromatherapy, and homeopathy.

I'm not requesting sick leave because my soul aches and I can't work.

I'm not giving up bathing and eating.

I'm not taking to drink.

I'm not taking up cigarettes.

I'm not going to drag myself around the street.

I'm not wearing the expression of a foolish abandoned woman.

Olga smiled at me, and I felt like crying on her shoulder or between her commodious breasts. I wanted her to stroke me and coddle me.

Since our conversation about the job of department head, she hadn't asked me anything more. She figured me for the sort that has to think everything through slowly, but I was ready with an answer now.

"I think I can do it, at least till you get back. You have to explain it all very well and give me the contact info for everyone I'll have to deal with," I told her, scared half to death but wanting to give it a try.

"It'll go fine, sweetie, everybody will love you. I'll give you all the instructions and I'll make sure you know how to find me, too. You'll see how well it will go. Just like your presentation of Daniel Arco."

I didn't cry into Olga's soft shoulder nor between her commodious breasts. I didn't tell her anything. We went into the meeting where she announced that I'd be the new department head for a time. I was glad to have made friends with the secretary, to a degree, since secretaries are the key people in these situations. Everyone else looked at me and applauded, making their calculations about whether I'd be a timorous substitute or a tyrannical control freak.

I got home and reviewed the latest events. Within just a few weeks, Marcos had left, I had broken up with Daniel, and I'd become temporary department head. I washed my hands and drank some water while I thought that over and listened to the calls.

The mechanic had finished the repairs and had made appointments with possible buyers. He wanted to know whether he was authorized to negotiate on the price in case someone asked for a discount.

Lorena invited me to a party to celebrate her anniversary and an offer of an exhibition in Mexico City, at the national university. "I don't want to hear any excuses or to have to come drag you over here," her speech ended. Sergio announced he was coming over for us to talk. "I love you and I want you to be okay, Marian," he whispered at the end.

Marcos's mother threatened to come over someday to have another coffee with me. Probably she wanted to bring me up to date on Marcos's string of successes in London, I thought.

The telephone rang. I was sure it would be Daniel.

"He's gone, Marian," Adrián began. "I just got back from the airport. God knows how much I tried to get him to tell you himself, but he wouldn't give in. He kissed me, for the first time, before he went through security. But though I dreamed of a kiss many times, I know it wasn't for me. So I have something that belongs to you. I'm not the ideal person to ask you to forgive him. But I dare do that and more, because what I want to say to you is that you should wait for him. Or we'll both wait for him, if you'd like to see me sometime. . . ."

Adrián was talking to the machine, which I figured was easier for him. I interrupted.

"Thank you Adrián. We'll talk later," I said.

I felt that sorrow was a disease with clinical symptoms, a very strong pain in the esophagus, a shrinking in, becoming less, freezing up. A fear. For oneself, at one's own brink.

ABSENCE

I had already experienced a sense of loss. My mother had died. All the time she was ill, I knew that her disease was not a steep stairway toward cure but a painful corridor toward death, yet still something inside me never accepted that. I could not get myself to believe that one day she would be no more. I lived each day like an exhausted soldier in an isolated trench, having lost all sense of time.

When she died, I still didn't understand, even though I took her hand and watched her go. Nor at the funeral, surrounded by people who sympathized with me; nor at the cemetery, keeping her company all the way to the place she'd never leave.

In the days following her death I felt liberated, weightlessly sad and strange. Everyone was surprised by my readiness to change things in her room, to get rid of her clothes and medicines and the objects that had been the props and scenery of her illness. I was a daughter who handled her sadness very well, knowing she had done everything in her power to care for her mother. And this daughter, proud of her good heart, had no guilty conscience and could allow herself to seek out a path toward happiness.

Then one day I realized that my mother had died and left me alone. I collapsed. I begin to pretend she was there in the kitchen to hear my remarks. I began to dream of her every night and evoke her in every drifting cloud or accustomed sound. I tried to do penance for the sin of having forgotten that she could die. I wallowed in the punishment of missing her, denying myself pleasures and the chance to get control of myself as everyone advised. My mother deserved all this. Trying to be happy felt to me like a betrayal.

Daniel got me to renounce this vow of sorrow. I forgot about suffering for my mother in return for all she had sacrificed for me. I was happy and passionate, I fought to keep him, I felt manipulated and jealous. I allowed myself earthly feelings, far removed from sacred duties. With his tricks and laughter, Daniel offered me a hand and pulled me back to the real world.

His departure did not send me back to the realm of mourning and the dead. Instead, his loss became my real loss. It taught me that my mother's absence was permanent and irremediable, while this new one involved something that that made it even harder to bear. Waiting.

WAITING

Depression is the frustration that follows anxiety. The lack of courage to accept unmet desires and unanswered prayers. Anxiety is waiting, uncertainty. Depression is when D-Day comes but the Allies do not land. Waiting comes to an end, replaced by certainty in the form of a No, a guarantee that everything will continue just as our anxiety had led us to fear. Depression signifies that anxiety has not been relieved.

There is a solution. Stop waiting. Don't dream, don't fantasize. Enjoy the peace of our daily routine, the air that yields us oxygen, the water that slakes our thirst. Close the doors on Peter Pan's island and Alice's gardens. Forget the ray of light, close the door, darken the windows, and banish all thought of annunciations.

As a sadistic practice, I went to the Malecón for a form of shock therapy. I wanted the sea to be sad, I wanted rain, I wanted the streets to miss him. Nothing of the sort. The waters seemed those of some clean, transparent shore, the clouds broke apart joyously in the blue, playing their games with a sun that radiated pride in the light that lit up the sky.

I sat on the wall, looking out at the *mare nostrum*. I remembered Daniel saying that the waves of the Malecón were also the waves of the Atlantic Ocean, never mentioning the Caribbean Sea. He liked to think we were part of something bigger.

You've been my storyteller, and I've been your attentive listener. My storyteller, juggler, bard, griot. My Scheherazade who makes every night into a starry sky and the bed into a magic carpet. Streetwise liar, trickster, survivor. Full of life, and too good to last. All this I confessed to a Daniel made of untiring, unceasing waves.

"Are you Spanish?" an older woman asked me, giving me a curious look. I shook my head no, not wanting to talk. I was sad and didn't want to emerge from my sadness.

"French?"

I shook my head again, surprised by her persistence in assigning me other nationalities.

"So you're Cuban?" she continued.

This time I nodded tiredly. I told her yes and started to get up.

"But from Havana or Miami?"

"What do you want?" I asked, finally curious.

"I have a serving set made of Sèvres porcelain. I'm looking for someone to sell it to." She seemed happy that I had answered, and embarrassed that she'd interrupted me.

I reached into my purse and found my antique dealer's card.

She looked at me as if she couldn't believe it. Eyes riveted on the card, she offered her thanks.

I decided to go home. When I walked in, I neither washed my hands nor took a drink of water. I sat down to write the scene that had just passed on the Malecón. *Bonjour Tristesse*. The first vignette.

"The journey of those who leave only begins with that flight to Europe. That's the beginning, Marian, that idea of leaving this island, seeing the rest of the world, which although it is something that some Cubans do, practically none of us plan on it." So P.T. began his lecture the day he came to collect Lorena's paintings, though I suspected that his visit was as much about therapy, the service friends are always willing to offer.

"People are so eager to travel that they worry about what

will go wrong. Flights delayed, questions posed by officials in the airport before stamping the exit permit. The journey before the journey is so exhausting, you end up worrying you won't be able to go after all.

"Then, on the airplane, the 'rest of the world' from which you feel so isolated begins. You don't know how to buckle your seatbelt, you're intimidated by the stewardess, you don't know which things she offers are free and which you have to pay for. And once you land, there on the other side, you can spend a long time learning about insurance, or how to use an ATM machine.

"You're dazzled by the well-dressed women, the men in suits and ties heading out with their briefcases every morning. You eat everything you've dreamed about, in the quantities you've dreamed of too.

"But the rest of the world lives real life too. You start looking for a job. You get to know the city inside out, but it still feels strange and you haven't made any friends. You start remembering, and the memories pen you in and suck you dry. You realize how beautiful your country and your people are. You start worshipping an ideal Havana that lives in your heart, while you resign yourself to living outside it."

"Or you don't need that. Daniel doesn't fit into that picture of crushing nostalgia," I said.

"Those who have gone need us more than we need them," he answered. "Our needs can be taken care of with a few dollars. What they need can't be stuffed into a handful of letters.

"Finally, one day comes the long-awaited first visit back," P.T. went on, like a visionary in a trance. "You're here, but you're not from here. You find Havana as foreign as Jakarta. You think you want to go home. But wasn't this your home? You don't belong anywhere anymore. In the airport they don't ask you so many questions. But you ask yourself questions, and the answers take a long time and lots of tears."

"I can't imagine Daniel pining for the life he had here."

"That life was made up of you, his friend, a Havana full of books, time to write, and his skills as a happy vagabond. Believe me, wherever he is now he doesn't have much time for Whitman or Lorca. When two Cubans meet up outside of Cuba, the first thing they ask each other is, 'How long have you been here?'"

"Sounds like a conversation between prisoners."

P.T. nodded and got up to leave.

"Don't miss the party. Lorena won't forgive you."

"Don't worry, I'm coming."

Daniel is in the Prado, looking at Las Meninas and discovering in the original painting something he's never seen before. His eyes are tearing up before such grandeur. Or he's in the Alhambra by night, seeing his reflection in the fountain in the Court of the Lions, surrounded by genies and princesses. I'm here, imagining him. Torn between all my good wishes for him and a hope that things won't go so well for him there without me. These were my thoughts as I watched P.T. leave my building with the rolled-up canvases under his arm, accompanied by the violet light of dusk.

IT'S SEVEN A.M. THE *bus stop is packed. People hold onto the habit of trying to get to work whether the Ministry of Transport cooperates or not. There's a small man. He's got a boy's build and a dreamy look on his face. He's one of those people who are only slightly Downs, who make you think their only problem is an excess of goodness and faith. He's waiting for the bus, keeping tight hold of a folder full of papers. He got here before anyone else. He's the first in line, at the head of a queue that, with the wait, has gotten wider than it is long. He's never learned how to board a seven a.m. bus. The rest know how. The bus chugs off, leaving him staring at the passengers, all those who had gotten on ahead of him, who left him outside. His expression clears, he straightens up, holding tight to his folder. Once again, he's first in line, waiting for the next bus. Behind him, a new line gets wider and more disorderly as the wait goes on. Bonjour Tristesse.*

MARCOS'S MOTHER GAVE ME an ostentatious kiss and came in,

feigning embarrassment so as to make me feel uncomfortable and, therefore, very friendly.

I did as expected, asking after Marcos.

"Marian, my dear, the truth is that I'm so happy I wanted to come tell you right away because I know you'll be happy too. Marcos is coming back to Havana."

"Really??" My surprise was not put on, much to her delight.

"They've offered him a management job here. In a joint venture with a Canadian firm that has branches all over the world."

I've never been envious. But I wondered, honestly, who was tossing the dice up there in such a way that some people always came out so much on top, while others were always left out.

"Marcos is very intelligent," she declared with a smile. "Why should he play second fiddle in a foreign country when he can contribute so much to his own?"

I marveled at the way Marcos's mother could identify what would be good for her son with what would be good for the nation.

"I'd be so happy if you two got back together. You were always my favorite. I'm among those who believe in 'birds of a feather, flock together.'"

I agreed, smiling. In situations like this, I've always been her favorite, because I've always sat still for her broadsides.

"But, from what I've been hearing, you've got someone else. Are things working out okay with him?"

"Yes, quite well."

"I'm so glad to hear that, Marian. Is he a professor at the university?"

"He's a writer."

"Writers always have their heads in the clouds. You need somebody more practical, a man you can rely on. Life in Cuba demands someone who's always on his toes. But Marcos will always be your friend, you know that, don't you? He loves you, I mean, we both do. You know you can always count on us."

"Yes, I know, thank you. And you can count on me."

"Now, dear, with this post Marcos will be taking up, they'll be checking into his social and political qualifications, to make sure of his appropriateness and reliability. They have to be sure he won't betray the country's interests. So, I gave your contact information, as someone who could serve as a reference. I hope that's not a bother."

Finally. I thought she'd never get to the purpose of her visit. I'm an honest citizen and I fulfill my civic duties and I'm a university professor, an acting department head. I look upstanding, discreet, and friendly. Perfect for making a good impression on those who would be checking up on her son.

"Don't worry. You did the right thing. I'll be happy to help Marcos out."

"And he feels the same. He already told me he's dying to see you. That wouldn't create any problem for you, would it?"

"Of course not. He can come here whenever he wants."

"Thank you, my dear. You're as lovely as ever. You know I want the best for you, though I'd have preferred for you to stay with us. Well, God disposes."

She gave me a kiss on each cheek, Spanish style. She shook her head to ruffle the perfect curls that framed her eternally triumphant face. Was a mother like this a requirement for things to go well in one's life, I wondered as I watched her descend the steps as if walking down the broad stairs of the Houses of Parliament.

THE TWO WOMEN BEHAVE *like actresses in a spicy play, taking offense with nearly sensual anger, expressed through obscene gestures and curse words. They are old, strong, and lively.*

It seems like a settling of scores, a trial carried out on the street. One shouts at the other, "Bitch, robber, you took what belongs to me."

People stop in their tracks, no one in this city is in such a hurry that they'll miss a good fight. The crowd swirls around them. Two actresses in an amphitheater, a Havana stage.

It could be a fight over a man, as in tragedies and comedies, operas and operettas, vaudeville and daily life.

One of them decides to exit the stage. She casts a mocking glance at the crowd and asks them to make room. A passage opens and she, the thief of the farce, proudly walks off.

The other, the one robbed, pursues her—first with taunts and then hurrying her steps to catch up. They start fighting, grabbing each other by the hair.

The spectators do what they always do in such cases—divide themselves arithmetically into equal groups to grab hold of the contestants and separate them.

Finally, the source of the dispute, up to then unknown, enters the scene. Making itself known, taking center stage as in the soliloquy of the last act, a yellow umbrella appears. Everyone laughs. Some clap. As in a morality play, the virtuous win and the guilty are punished. The umbrella's legitimate owner recovers possession, straightens her clothes and her hair, and acknowledges the public with a flirtatious bow. She opens her yellow umbrella and, in a circle of yellow light, departs.

The show is over and the group disperses. Everyone goes back to what they were doing a few minutes before, heading where they were heading while discussing what they've just seen. Just like a cultured audience on its way out of the theater.

"I've never gone to bed with anyone who hasn't been able to pay. 'Yours for richer or for poorer' isn't in my vocabulary."

Adrián and I were in an Italian-style *paladar* on the top floor of a Central Havana apartment building. The private restaurant had four tables, occupied mostly by foreigners.

The waiters and some customers were acquainted with Adrián. We sat down at the only empty table. Adrián pulled out my chair and opened the curtains of a picture window. All we could see was sea and sky, as if we were in the dining room of a cruise ship in a film.

I don't know real Italian food, just the pizza, lasagna,

cannelloni and spaghetti that populated the self-service pizzerias that satisfied our adolescent hunger in the seventies and eighties, one on every corner, with names like Vita Nuova, Buona Sera, and Cinecittà.

Or those with greater pretensions, tablecloths, waiters, and some delicacies: La Romanita, Montecatini, Castel Nuovo. Those had risotto and tiramisu as well.

But *parmigiano reggiano, carpaccio,* and *torta della nonna* had never appeared on any menu I had seen.

I read the menu, which was endless. I looked at the prices and opted for the cheapest, a Margherita, but Adrián smiled and said no. He spread the menu before me while covering the prices with his hand. He warned me that I could not choose a Margherita.

Adrián was behaving like the shy rich man, or a famous one who was trying to stay out of the limelight without giving offense, in a spot where everyone was intent on greeting and smiling at him.

He must have come here often with Daniel, they must have hatched plans and laughed like boys, telling beautiful and horrible things and promising what we've all promised someone, sometime.

"I don't know what to choose. Could you recommend something for me?"

Adrián requested a tasting sample of the whole menu, so as to teach me the basics. He assured me I would like it all.

"This way, the next time you come, you know what you want. The cook is a Cuban who lived in Rome for a long time and worked in a *trattoria.* He really learned his stuff."

"And then he came back," I put in.

I knew that everything I said had a second meaning. My unconscious betrayed my obsession with linking everything to Daniel.

"Yes. On one of his vacations in Havana he met the owner of this apartment. For a number of years they just saw each other during vacations, till they opened this restaurant, which now is quite well known. As you can see, it's got a group of steady customers, all the ones I said hello to."

"Haven't you ever thought about leaving? With all your contacts, it would be easy, I think."

"I don't know anyone abroad well enough to leave the place where I feel secure and control my own life. I don't want to be in some other city where I'm somebody's prisoner and spend the day shut up in an apartment watching cable TV and eating popcorn, without documents or friends. I'll wait till Daniel becomes famous to do my sightseeing in the rest of the world."

"But you could find a job."

"I have a job, Marian. For years I've been coming home in the mornings after working all night, with pouches under my eyes that feel like they're drooping to my knees, but money in my pocket every time. That money takes care of all my tastes, from buying expensive perfumes to giving old editions of books to my friends and their girlfriends."

There was no boastfulness in that, more a sense of pride in having fulfilled some promise he made to himself.

I wanted to ask whether he had ever been in love, but I didn't think his telling me about his work gave me the right to pry into his emotional life.

"I'm friendly toward them," he went on. "I put up with their neuroses, depressions, anxieties, and obsessions. I'm happy when good things happen to them. I cheer them up over the bad things. And I charge."

"Like a psychoanalyst," I joked.

We had progressed to dessert. Adrián said that to finish off we would have a liqueur, Amaretto or Limoncetto ". . . etto, etto," he laughed.

Daniel, just look what you're missing, I thought over and over. The two people who love you the best, seated at a window filled with the sea.

"Look, here's a guide to Madrid I requested for you." He

handed me a book with a photo of La Cibeles on the front. "I leafed through it already, I was curious. You'll be able to imagine Daniel, where he is."

Daniel came into our conversation along with the liqueurs. This also brought the moment when I could ask.

"You've heard from him, haven't you?"

"Yes." The statement ended there. Adrián didn't feel that my question required a longer answer.

"Is he okay?"

"I don't know, Marian. The sound was bad and he was nervous, he wanted to tell me things and listen at the same time. It was raining and there was static. It was hard."

"Did he ask about me?"

"Yes. I told him you were fine, that you knew he had gone, and that I was sure I'd see you."

"He didn't give you any message?"

Adrián weighed his desire to soothe me against his friendship for Daniel. His desire to give me some good news that afternoon and his vow of silence. Finally he found a phrase to offer me.

"He says that the bananas there are more expensive and not as good."

MADRID WAS BUILT BY Philip II in the center of Spain. It's far from the sea, and the river that flows through it is insignificant.

Everyone descended from Spaniards needs to visit the city. A hundred and ten years ago, we were Spaniards too.

Like a calendar, Madrid has four seasons. At least since Franco's time, however, it doesn't get a snowfall worthy of the name. The summer heat is dry and exhausting. Everyone escapes from the city, which becomes populated by flocks of Germans and Scandinavians carrying little bottles of water. In the fall it rains a lot, people walk hurriedly underneath their umbrellas, and since the city is always under reconstruction, the streets become mired in a mix of rain and cement.

Since it's true that a hundred and ten years ago we were Spaniards too, we go there. Perhaps to seek in the past some present-day help in building our future.

Then we discover that the habit of colonizing and catechizing is still going strong. No one gives you a decent job. If you're a woman and you stand still for two minutes in the street, someone will offer to pay you to suck him off in the Casa de Campo. If you want to make friends, your options are the Chinese who are always working, the Moroccans who hang out on the corner, or Bulgarians who won't speak with anyone.

Madrid is always in a hurry. The best place to find a smile and a bit of space is in the lowest class of bars, where, drunk as everyone is, you might be mistaken for one of the princesses of the realm.

Madrid is a city where you expect good things to happen to you because a hundred and ten years ago we were all Spaniards. But that's not enough.

Madrid is full of ladies with square-heeled shoes and hairdos out of *Tootsie*, carrying shopping bags from El Corte Inglés and gossiping on and on. Police who graduated from Francoist schools and rich kids who go to great lengths to appear American. People who were once taught in school that a hundred and ten years ago we were all Spaniards, but have now forgotten that completely.

MADRID IS AN ISLAND, surrounded by a warm sea that sometimes, in the morning, rises into the streets and bathes the feet of pedestrians in the froth of little waves.

The center of Madrid is a canal that empties into the sea. In the canal are gondolas, canoes, and sailboats. Travelers eat the plentiful salmon, herring, sardines, and shellfish whose colors and shapes come from the imagination of Hieronymus Bosch.

Many bridges cross the canal. Of wood and marble, full of statues, lampposts, arches, and free shops that distribute happiness, health, success.

There are wide boulevards, monumental plazas, bohemian hideaways, labyrinthine alleys, sumptuous buildings, and skyscrapers ranging from baroque to modernist to futuristic. In all of them, the windows are full of flowers.

A thousand languages are spoken in Madrid, where any tongue is understood. A smile is the Esperanto of the city. The people are variegated and dress in different colors. There are rainbows though it doesn't rain, there are Northern Lights and nights clothed in white. At sunset, the bells of the churches, mosques, and temples all ring, and the people kneel down in the sand to pray to the God of their neighbors, asking for the neighbors to be blessed.

The people drink in bars, in gardens, in pubs, in bistros, at kiosks. In the street, the subway, the banks, on the grass. In offices, in the parliament, in cathedrals. In the woods, parks, and plazas.

And they dance. It's always Carnaval in Madrid. People undulate and sway with their faces masked. The street people are costumed as bankers, the illegal immigrants as senators, the soldiers as hippies. The line of dancers moves in a great wave of pleasure, infinite and inexhaustible, toward heaven as painted by Velázquez.

I didn't open Adrián's guidebook to Madrid and to Daniel. I set it down next to the telephone, in that corner of the New World.

THIS TIME THERE WERE no surprises. Sadness has that advantage, it holds still. I got dressed for Lorena's party in full knowledge that this time Daniel would not appear. I wouldn't be waiting for him, his absence would not make me anxious, we wouldn't fight and he wouldn't tell me any lies. We wouldn't make love.

It was a hot night so I decided to walk along the Malecón. But there wasn't any breeze, not even by the sea.

Lorena's house is large and solid, built at the turn of the twentieth century. One of those with decorative grates around the windows and columns at the entranceway. Lorena was born there and won't hear a word about moving. She dreams of her sons marrying good women, of the sort who no longer exist, and founding families who will live happily in those same hallways, treading the antique tiled floors and brushing against the discolored walls.

For the party, she had pulled the electric fans out of all the bedrooms and scattered them around so they disheveled everyone's hair and added some ventilation to that of the windows opened to the warm, humid night.

The house was packed. Lorena knows how to mix colors, flavors, and people.

We gave each other massive hugs. I told her, without words, all that was happening to me, and she listened to the words I didn't say. We went into the kitchen, where she told me her news.

"I'm not going anywhere. I don't want to travel, not for three days and not to stay. I don't have time, and I don't have interest."

Lorena talked a blue streak. She was making one of her famous rice dishes and she circulated among pots, spices, and the most diverse ingredients, leftovers from previous meals that were resting in the expectation of being blended and ennobled in whatever invention would feed the many guests.

"Lorena, I don't get it, what nonsense is this? Everyone wants to travel, it's a normal desire, and especially here. Why are you passing up this opportunity? It will be good for you, from any point of view. They'll pay your expenses, Mexico is a quick flight, you'll be able to speak your own language and after a few days' break from routine you'll come home and something in you will have changed."

"I don't want anything in me to change, Marian. I don't want my kids to miss me, or for P.T. to have to take over chores that we generally split half and half. And there's everything that comes before the trip: paperwork, red tape, visa, exit permit, tickets, packing, money, getting the house ready for me to go. Then the trip: get up, smile, marvel, answer the same question a thousand times, walk, get tired out, sleep badly, eat weird things, and so on, until I board another plane which will bring me back to the place that I left a mess, where now I'll be wiped out, used up, and directionless."

"What about if everything goes very well, the arrangements turn out to be simple, you like Mexico, you make friends, they like your work, you find opportunities, and you come home full of stories to tell?" I proposed this other version without understanding what Lorena was driving at.

"I've thought about that too. In that case, my life will have turned to muck. Everybody here is more or less okay till they catch that first goddamn plane. Then wherever they go, any shithole of the earth, game over. Suddenly they're in crisis, overheated, and they can never live normally here again. They lose all ability to talk about anything else, they think travel is the only virtue that can do anything for them or that they respect in anyone else. All they do is think about the next trip. Instead of taking care of the present they spend their energy inventing a future that's about another seat in another airplane to go to some other shithole of the earth. All their minutes, days, hours, thoughts, and actions are devoted to this. No. However it turns out, I'd be fucked."

Lorena, blanketed in her apron and wielding an enormous ladle, stirred the kettle forcefully. Like a witch out of the Brothers Grimm.

"After the famous first voyage, I won't be an artist any more, just an anxious pre-traveler. I won't be able to concentrate on what I'm doing because all my neurons will be at the service of the famous second voyage, and then the third. No thanks. Leave me here in my corner. I don't want any surprises. I prefer to imagine that some things are still where they ought to be. I don't think everyone needs to travel. I think there are some people who can't be bothered with leaving their house."

"Fine. Then get yourself an agent who will handle your works and show them abroad. You'll be a mysterious Cuban artist who doesn't want to set foot outside Cuba. As a publicity stunt, that's not bad."

"No. An agent is someone who tells you to paint something different from what you want. I don't want to get mixed up with them. Look, somebody who likes their job doesn't neglect it for a hobby. Someone who loves their partner doesn't go looking for an affair. Someone who feels good in one place doesn't go sniffing out someplace else."

"Lorena, so many people in the world travel, and nobody comes to these conclusions. Traveling is good, it confers some humility as an antidote to the egocentrism we suffer on this island, it teaches you there are many ways to do things, that the world is big and different. You can't deny yourself a chance to see other lives, other cities."

"Marian, there are people who simply fuse with the landscape that belongs to them. People who inhabit the scenes that tourists take a glance at, and who give them the advice they need. People who show up in the photos of others, and come to be part of the description of this place or that. I'm that kind of people. I don't want to be a baffled tourist, making empty pilgrimages with a pocket guidebook, a digital camera, and a lot of hurry."

"What does P.T. say? He was happy about your trip."

"P.T. was happy about waving goodbye and about welcoming me back, you know his obsession with borders. He's told me travel stories from Sinbad to Conrad, but none of that convinces me. My two previous husbands left. I'm not leaving my kids even for a jaunt to Varadero. I'm not going to be an intermittent wife. What matters is being together in good times and in bad."

We laughed a lot over this, as we put the finishing touches on a rice plate full of surprises. Lorena is way too atheistic to be citing matrimonial sacraments. She believes in things that find their way into her head, as long as they don't come from any religion. She says anybody who's on the right side of God doesn't need to be making dates with him in any church.

We changed the topic. Lorena was my friend who didn't want to leave, and I was happy with that. Who wanted to be here always. By choice, not by inexorability.

I took the same route home as I had when coming to the party, but now the breeze had risen and the residents of Havana were rushing to take up their positions on the seawall. I like this city, I wanted to say out loud. To Daniel.

There are days I haven't been waiting for you. Days when I've gone out and noticed how the sun and the sea don't need you, nor the city either; how thousands of oblivious pedestrians make their way through it, immersed in their daily travails and accomplishments, unaware that you exist and their lives not at all reduced by this lack. But then, when I notice that forgetting you for a few hours has been my only accomplishment for the day, I rebel against the idea of such a sacrifice. I'll remember you tomorrow, I vow when I switch off the bedside light at the conclusion of a TV movie that ends with corpses on both sides.

Sergio said it was normal for me to be sad and anxious, to cry and sleep badly. He took these for signs of life. Of life and of love, and to him love is always good, even in its downsides. But when I asked him about the future, what he thought would happen, he had no answer, which meant that anything was possible. I might decide to go to Madrid. Daniel might come back. We might forget each other.

"Don't try to rush things or force them," he advised me. "Don't hurry them up. Enjoy the role of chance. It's the best-organized thing there is."

I SHOULD RENT OUT one of the bedrooms, I said to myself while seated in the living room, totaling up how many square meters I owned. As Daniel had advised me, and as he had assured me I would never do. *You're not cut out to survive in this city, Marian,* were his words that I remembered. But maybe I was. I'd found a good reason to try.

If I rented, Daniel could come back and we could live here in some security, without persistent worries, and we'd even be able to buy ourselves some small treats. He would devote his time to writing, not taking on other jobs to pay the rent or the heating bill of his hypothetical European house. I would read his work and give him advice that he would decide wasn't worth taking. We'd be happy with every book he published, each one better than the one before.

I sat in my fragment of the city, fondling each of these dreams as if I were a milkmaid in fairy tale. And I tried to assess the potential value of the building where I've lived since I was born.

The building was dirty. Someone had thrown up on the stairway, presumably someone who'd gotten drunk in the nightclub in the basement. Once upon a time we'd entertained ourselves circulating petitions to have the club closed and turned into a library or sex education center or a place for floral therapy, but it seemed that the best therapy and most effective form of culture was dancing. Anyway, the vomit was just a temporary detail on top of the permanent debris, the cigarette butts, candy wrappers, dirt, mud, and shoe tracks.

I don't know how many people have been hired to clean the building over the years. Always too old to climb eight stories with a bucket and mop in hand. Sooner or later they quit, and then sooner or later another old woman appears, another who's trying to get by on a small pension and doesn't want to depend on her kids. Or her kids don't want her to depend on them.

And since we're in the Third World already, we can't import people to do the jobs we don't like. We've got thought patterns of the First World and an economy of the Third. We used to import people from other provinces who would do the work Havanans scorned, but now immigration from the provinces is controlled. Havana is overcrowded. It seems we have no room even for those of us already here.

So, the building stays dirty. Someday soon, we'll all resign ourselves to cleaning the hallways and the stairs and so we'll get the place clean. And then it will get dirty again, and so on and on until another old woman arrives with bucket and mop.

The cleaning issue shouldn't be an obstacle to my renting out my mother's room, I thought. I could clean my flight of the public stairs, too.

The next issue was the neighbors. If I were to decide to rent without a license, I'd have to depend on their complicity. I took a quick inventory of those who lived above, below, and across from me—with whom I can never seem to agree. Maybe that's just because they're my neighbors. I imagined a building full of friends, but I wasn't sure that our harmony and friendship would last very long if we were in such close quarters.

On the second floor there was a large family in which, until recently, nobody worked. They were all sick, on leave without pay, or in between jobs. They spent their time shopping or hanging out, going to physical therapy or standing in lines. They were supported by regular remittances from a distant cousin who'd been living in Miami for many years. They celebrated Christmas with turkey and *turrones*, and they ordered even their aspirin from Miami, since they were sure that everything from there must be better. They were always up on the latest fashions and knew every discotheque and boutique.

Then the Miami cousin decided to come spend a Christmas with her loving and dependent relatives. For the first few days, it seemed normal to her that no one got up before ten a.m., after which all were content to go shopping and eat out. It was Christmas, after all. But then the holiday passed and the relatives' schedules did not change. Puzzled, she asked when vacation ended, which uncorked litany of orthopedic issues, psychological ailments, problematic bosses, pursuit of better jobs, and, at last, the happy assurance that all this was possible because she was supporting them.

The cousin then explained the source of the money that

allowed them such uninterrupted leisure. In the early mornings she cleaned a building, then she took care of an old woman until eight at night, and on the weekends she cleaned private homes. This vacation was her first in six years. She didn't think she could afford another for quite a while.

So the juicy remittances came to an end. The cousin was not hard-hearted enough to turn off the spigot completely, but the family had to cut back their spending, and a few of them even found work.

After visits to Vienna and Berlin, solo organ performances in Gothic cathedrals as a self-styled messenger from the angels, the musician on the third floor set off for far eastern Cuba in search of mystical experiences like those of the Beatles in India. Two months later, he came back with a dancer of native origin. That was how we discovered there were still a few communities remaining in Cuba that lived in stilt houses, ate *casabe* made from yucca flour, and danced the *areítos* of old.

We all attended their wedding service in the nearby church, desirous as we were of seeing this girl who had stepped out of a Gauguin painting draped in a white gown full of ruffles and ribbons, down the back and shoulders of which poured a shining cascade of blue-black hair. She gazed upon the unmoving saints and listened to the sacramental recitations with a smile that might have been innocence or might have been craftiness, it was hard to say.

A few weeks later, her relatives began to arrive, but they had trouble adjusting. Instead of taking advantage of the much-touted virtues of the capital, they longed for places where they could see the sun and swim in a river worth the name. They wanted to eat healthy things that were not manufactured in unknown places, and they were tired of being put on edge by the harsh noises emitted by doorbell, telephone, television, and stereo.

Nonetheless, they spent hours listening to the musician, sitting like statues as he poured out minuets and preludes by Bach. Finally, they nodded in approbation and continued in their silence.

But little by little they began trickling back to their village, and they spoke of taking the girl with them, as the musician glumly confided in me.

The dancer's family found everything very aggressive, but each day it grows harder to evade the neuroses of modernity. I don't know how long their oasis of peace will last. The suppliers of false comforts, of fast cars and cell phones with camera and vibrator, the eternal manufacturers of anything and everything are committed to evangelizing all of the poor souls who lack computers or DVDs.

My closest neighbor is the hero. His name is in the history books and his house is full of commendations and historic photos in black-and-white or sepia. He's an authentic hero. He doesn't talk about the feats he supposes we have all read about. The hero's first wife was his hometown sweetheart, the one who feared for his life, waited for him while he was in prison, hid his incriminating documents, and gave him children. She took care of the house so he could make Revolution in his position as a hero with heavy responsibilities.

The hero's second wife was his secretary, somewhat younger and very enthusiastic. An emancipated woman, she smoked cigarettes and imprisoned her attractive rear end in very tight pants. She grew to know so much about the hero's life as to constitute his memory. She stayed up late at night typing and writing letters, slept on the sofa in the office because with only a few hours' break there was no point in going home. She converted the hero's office into a home so welcoming that the hero stopped going to his own house or talking to his wife.

The hero's third and current wife is very young. She hasn't done anything for the hero, whom she met while researching historical events in old magazines for a paper she was writing in her first year of college. One day this brave and sweet gentleman gave her a lift to class, and she ended up attached to him. In spite of what one might expect, she has been very faithful. Instead of making the old hero ridiculous by clothing him in the attire of a young person determined to keep up with the times, she has begun to dress like an older woman. She gathers her hair into a severe bun, wears strings of small pearls, and dresses in ageless outfits. She speaks slowly and walks at his pace. The joke among the neighbors is that the hero will have a fourth wife soon, because this one has grown too old for him.

The hero's wife's best friend is the very old woman on the fifth floor. In 1961, she met Jackie Onassis while her name was still Kennedy. They shared a meal in La Côte Basque, where she got a waiter to take a snapshot. When she returned to Havana a few years later, she began to live off the photo and the memory, and by now she's milked them all for every dried-up drop. She's served as consultant for research on the Missile Crisis, Martin Luther King and the civil rights movement, Manhattan tourist guides, and biographies of Truman Capote. She's more of a fixture on TV than the guy who does the weather forecast. She travels a lot, is interviewed constantly, gives lectures on the Kennedys, the sixties, New York architecture, Woodstock, and the short story as practiced in the United States. She even has a website and a fan club. The first thing you see on walking into her apartment is her smiling face—ever more faded and blurry—alongside the lovely ex-first-lady in the photo that changed her life.

In the penthouse live the "gusanos" who never managed to leave. Since 1959 they've been declaring that their family stays out of politics, and they've been very consistent about isolating themselves from everything that's gone on. They remember the names of every brand of American breakfast cereal that used to be in the store. But, curiously, none of them has left the country. They don't have any relatives in the U.S. to request their visas, and they have no opportunities to go abroad on work duties and not come back.

Instead they've become patriots of another age, worshipping the Constitution of 1940 and Estrada Palma's administration of 1902. They're very proper, and they maintain a home in the style of the fifties, so visiting them is a kind of trip into the Twilight Zone. Everyone says they're super boring but unfailingly polite. They still open the elevator door for you and help you with your heavy things. Completely *démodé*.

And on the first floor live the girls. They frequent the gym by day and the discos by night, not going anywhere except by car. Nocturnal animals who sleep till noon and always emerge with smiles and shining hair.

I decided I had nothing to fear from any of the neighbors. None of them would inform on me just because a few days a month a stranger, carrying a bottle of water and burned red by our tropic sun, might venture in and out of my house muttering in bad Spanish and smiling at all the world. I told myself I would give it some thought.

I READ THE LATEST vignette, just finished, aloud. I wondered whether I'd been able to tell what I'd seen, and whether readers would feel what I had tried to describe.

My relationship to Literature has always been that of a book-worm. I taught myself to read with a bit of help from my mother, who then began offering me books. They became my best friends, always at hand to give me a boost, asking nothing except my time and my desire to devote it to them. For me, books have provoked more emotions and sensations than real life. And they've always accompanied it.

I chose to savor and pick apart what others wrote. I majored in Language and Literature, almost unable to believe that I could get a university degree for doing my most favorite thing.

After graduation I stayed on inside the same buildings and classrooms, repeating the things I had repeated to myself as an undergraduate. Now aloud, from the lectern and writing on the chalkboard, for my students.

To keep up the spirits of my dying mother, I pretended to be writing a book. The book became more pressing than the disease, more soothing than the medications, more agreeable than reality. We got a lot of enjoyment out of a novel of which I never even wrote the first word.

Before Daniel came into my life, *The Eskimo* preceded him. I read his words without having seen his face. My first sense of his voice was from writing, not speech. I met him through his book, and Literature was the cause of our first argument. The argument that led to us reconciling as friends and then turned us into lovers.

His idea about our writing a book together was our last mirage, our last plan without departures or separations. A plan that envisioned us together, doing many things.

Now, writing my part of *Bonjour Tristesse* was like dancing a *pas de deux* without a *partenaire*, like conversing solo or masturbating without fantasies. Like living without Daniel.

I'M WALKING BEHIND TWO brothers. They're old men, and one of them is retarded. It's apparent that the other has taken care of him since they were children. That he has devoted his life to this task. That they have no resources and don't know anyone. That this is no trick, that they are poor and honest. The older brother carries an ancient briefcase that seems to be his treasure. He guides the younger brother. It's always been that way. They've never asked God for an explanation.

Every smile of the child-brother provides an answer from the father-brother. They do not think about accomplishments, ambitions, or crowning projects. They move serenely though the streets that make up their little planet, thankful for things we are unable to taste.

FOR ME, LITERATURE WAS a bridge on which I walked alongside and toward my loved ones. But it didn't prove solid enough. My mother died despite her enthusiasm for the novel I invented for her. Daniel left in spite of his book and the one we were going to write together.

I tried to turn Literature into my tangled path toward happiness, a charm that would ward off departures and solitude, because in and of itself it was no longer enough to buffer me.

Thus I asked from it the three gifts that we hope our fairy godmothers will provide, the three wishes of folk tales and of life, the sound track of every toast at every holiday ritual, but no less heartfelt for their repetition: health, wealth, and love.

But Literature granted me none of these. My mother died. My salary is laughable in today's Havana. Daniel left me to go make Literature somewhere else.

On my computer screen, I reread all the vignettes, from the first one up to the words composed only a few minutes ago. I placed the cursor on the final period and held down the backspace key. Like an open mouth snaking backward, nothingness devoured each letter and space, leaving phrases half-completed and then continuing to gobble them until they disappeared. Every word became a senseless monosyllable and then nothing at all, until finally the cursor reached the first capital letter I had typed on the first day. And it deleted that too.

Eyes on the screen, now as blank as it had been before I began, as blank as many days ago, I was seized by a utopian fantasy common to scientists and mystics: to travel in time. To go back to the beginning and start over. Change history. Do it all differently. Delete the past. As if time were neither irreversible nor unidirectional.

In truth I had changed something. I was again who I had been before, the person who did not write. I had broken my part of something with Daniel.

But, even though I wouldn't be writing the book that he had forgotten all about, I was still waiting for him.

WHEN MARCOS CAME IN, my living room swirled with scents I hadn't known existed. Something about his forehead suggested he'd been doing a lot of thinking over the past few months. Though his eternal security was intact, his movements were not so dominating. He didn't bring me flowers or candies but a poster advertising the first performance of *Peter Pan* on December 27, 1904, in the Duke of York's Theatre.

"There's no place like your own country," he said, standing on my porch and looking out at the rain. "Not even the rain is the same somewhere else."

True enough. Especially when the possessive "your" is expansive and real. Coming home through the front door is a very fine thing to do. Enjoying all the good stuff: the sun, the sea, the people, and the security of knowing the shortcuts and hiding places, all the ins and outs. Having your problems taken care of, being freed of worries about money, food, transportation, shelter, or even vacations and travel. Those last two are problems a large slice of the population doesn't have, since they've never expected much in that regard.

I can't think of a better life, anywhere in the world, than the good life here and now.

All those ideas passed through my mind, but I didn't voice a word of them. I could save my breath with Marcos, because it was as if we spoke two different languages. His reflections didn't stimulate mine.

By contrast, I was always hanging on what came out of Daniel's mouth. Everything he said moved something inside me. For him, I always had answers and questions.

"How was London? Did you like it?"

"No. Everything you've read, seen, and heard is true. It's gray, rainy, and the churches are pretentious."

"Yes, that's clear from the movies. Don't you have any more personal impressions, now that you've lived there awhile?"

"Yes. The impressions of a foreigner with a middle-size business in the midst of a city that feels like a planet. You see all kinds of people and you think everyone must be welcome. Not so. The English understand who really belongs, and they let you know it. If you're not a blue-eyed Smith, then stay in your place and get used to it. We'll applaud your good manners while reminding you that you're not one of us. Do you know how many refugees from political conflicts there are in the world? Ten million. Europe is tired of them. Europe still has the pie, but it's getting smaller and smaller while more and more slices have to be cut. In spite of all their colonizing and exploitation, they don't think they owe anything to anybody. They say they've fought for what they have, which is why they're not as bad off as others. They're not very fond of being invaded by foreigners trying to make a living, working for less than themselves. They blame the foreigners for whatever goes wrong: violence, crime, low wages, and terrorism. I wouldn't be surprised to find us back in the days of segregated buses, like in Montgomery."

Not being a blue-eyed Smith must have hurt Marcos quite a bit, because otherwise racism and xenophobia would just be words out of left-wing periodicals to him. It wasn't that he didn't like London, but that he hadn't managed to conquer it. And now he was returning to a place where he could be powerful and well above average, the way his mother had taught him that one ought to live.

"It's all manipulation, the democracy of money," his diatribe against savage capitalism continued. "You assume that if you have a car and a cell phone, you're happy. To sustain that happiness, people put up with a lot. Don't believe the myth that everybody goes on vacation. Despite the famous European prosperity, there are people who barely make it to the end of the month, who lose their jobs and can't pay their bills, who one day find they're not middle class but jobless, with no future other than begging. Europe is in crisis. Naturally they don't want foreigners. They're afraid. Poverty always brings meanness of spirit."

Now I was listening closely, wondering whether these reflections were propelled, for the first time, by the good of Humanity and a fairer world—or whether, like so many times before, they were born of his desire for his own good, in a world as unjust as ever but on his side.

"Did you leave Monica because you couldn't stand London?"

"Yes. Well, I tried to convince her we should move someplace less aggressive where we'd feel more comfortable. But her family are used to being foreigners wherever they go. Or maybe if you're from the First World you're never a foreigner, even when you change countries. It's just us who are foreigners, when we leave the Third World for the First."

"It would be nice if the whole world were First. There would always be adventurous souls who changed where they lived, but that would just mean moving somewhere with different climate and customs." I tried to imagine a planet such as I had just described, but Marcos did not give me much time.

"I offered Monica's father a thousand ideas for entering much less competitive markets. I drafted prospectuses that would have made him a millionaire. But no, they're very stubborn. All I could get was a meeting of the board, where the vote went against me. That was the end of that."

"Democratic centralism. The minority has to obey the majority. We learned that in Marxism class," I said with a smile.

"Right. The fantasy that if you group a lot of stupid people together they make a smart one. How many visionaries do you know? How many people who are really geniuses are there in the world? Why should we pay attention to mediocrities? Just because there are more of them? Who's caused the world to progress, gray masses or individual geniuses? There are a few smart people, and then there's human stupidity, which is deep and wide. Does the common sense of the majority solve problems, or the inspiration of the few?"

"I don't believe in lone wolves who range so far ahead that their goals are invisible to the rest who come behind," I said. "There are lots of gray people, as you put it, working toward modest goals, who achieve things that eventually become great feats, accomplished slowly through mutual effort. It's all very well to design a pyramid, but if nobody takes on carrying the stones, it'll never really exist."

"You should have been a nun, Marian. Your resignation has always seemed to me like a preemptive rejection of anything good you could achieve in life. Losing before you start to play, accepting whatever comes. How are you doing, by the way?"

"I'm doing well. I'm here. Where everybody is like me. I have two last names, in Spanish, like everybody else. The thing is, here we don't look down on foreigners. We worship them instead."

Marcos laughed. Whatever he might say, he was happy. He had good things awaiting him, and the failed marriage didn't seem to bother him much. He said they weren't yet legally divorced. Maybe he was trying to decide whether that would be useful or not.

"Well, Marian, here I am again. For a while I'll be swamped with the new office and job and everything, but promise me that when I'm free, we'll have dinner. Did you know that in London the food is very bad?"

"No, I thought they only drank tea."

Marcos looked out at the rain and took a deep breath. Though his motives for coming back were most likely very calculated, he did like being here.

He took his leave, but not before commenting, "And your new friend? You haven't said anything about him." Old school as he is, Marcos couldn't manage any other word to refer to his successor.

"He's gone."

"Where to?"

"Madrid. Since then, no news," I added quickly, as if I had a lot of information I didn't want to share.

"He'll be back, you'll see."

He kissed me on the forehead and left.

No one had offered Daniel the co-directorship of a Canadian firm in Havana. He didn't have a mansion in a fine neighborhood and a pseudo-empress mother. Nor a wife with a pedigree and a family business. Perhaps he would be happy over there, if he could hold onto his dreams long enough to make them come true. Meanwhile, he'd say that the best things Spain had to offer were for everyone, like paintings and the streets. His Europe would be different, much less ambitious, I told myself while watching the raindrops thin out and disappear.

London is gruff and has no seacoast. I looked at Havana, bordered by miles of ocean, but for the first time I felt the water was besieging us. What we have is a wall where sea meets land, not a beach that one can walk from end to end, setting foot simultaneously in city and sea. What we can do is to look out over the waves, which exist as a promise of the rest of the world. But the promise is unreliable. Like Daniel's return.

I decided to go out.

THE SEA WAS FLAT, as if someone had spread a blanket over the water to put it to sleep. There were two suns, it seemed. One hung inside a long, grey stripe of sky, suspended immobile over the sea. The other was in the water painting a circle of orange light. The cloud-sun was dropping down to reunite with the sea-sun. As if someone up above had switched on a light, the city glowed yellow this Friday at six p.m.

Everyone who'd been waiting for the rain to stop rushed out of their workplaces. Lines of speeding cars filled both sides of the seaside drive, while some of the many trying to cross on foot made matador moves at them, much to the drivers' annoyance.

The seawall filled up rapidly. People sat looking at the dampened city, the sunset, and the curving Malecón flanked by sea on one side and shaky pastel-colored buildings on the other.

The people eyed each other. They were looking to sell and buy, to exchange friendly talk, to complain about the generally bad state of things. To say how fine these afternoon rains were for shaking off the heat. Or how, no matter how much it rained, nothing would change.

I took my seat in those bleachers. I always enjoyed the atmosphere after a rain.

A car slowed down and a woman opened the rear door in the

middle of four lanes of traffic. She dropped a puppy out. It was small and naked-looking.

"Damn, look at that!" shouted some boys next to me.

"What kind of sons of bitches would do that?"

"Should we grab it?"

"We won't have time."

"I can't watch," said the only girl in the group.

I followed the scene, hypnotized. The puppy was still in the middle of the road. Stupefied by the lights, noise, and traffic, it watched the car drive away. It was right on the yellow line. It tried to move, but couldn't. Trembling, it tried again. One car managed to avoid it with a suicidal swerving maneuver, and the dog returned to the yellow line, shaking. It kept going in that direction, into the path of a car whose driver was not as skillful or not as nice.

I closed my eyes to avoid seeing the end. The boys yelled and I knew it was all over. I wondered whether I could have written this up for the collection of sad events.

OLGA WAS SEATED IN my chair, smiling warmly, her complexion somewhere between white and pink, like the color of a Nordic baby's butt. She gave me a big hug, and I felt that something good was about to happen, some Viking energy she had brought back was going to change my life.

Everyone around us looked happy too, as if Olga and I were very special and everyone had been waiting to gawk at our reunion.

"Marian, I'm going to live in Reykjavik. The dean of the Foreign Language Faculty and I are getting married. That means I'll have to leave everybody. Will you miss me?"

This was truly unexpected. Olga, that adorable plump presence, my abundant angel who looked out for me even without knowing it? Did fat sixty-something women marry Icelanders? Would the head of the Spanish Language and Literature Department of the University of Havana go off and live someplace where they spoke a tongue that was half Swedish and half Latin?

"Do you know what everyone has told me? That you're stupendous as department head! They'll be delighted to work with you for the next two hundred years."

Everyone applauded and agreed. Their lives had been good during my administration, in which I demanded only that they teach their classes and give their exams, and they had done so. We had only a few meetings, in which I asked for whatever favors I wanted done, not ordering anyone to do them.

During that time, I learned that the verb *to solve* does not apply only to equations, riddles, and crossword puzzles. One also solves or resolves the issues of rentals at the beach, powdered milk, children's school uniforms, or appointments for an ultrasound.

I learned that the grammatical tense of this verb always implies *during working hours*. And finally, that this isn't anybody's fault.

Therefore, Q.E.D.

The verb *to solve*, when used in this grammatical tense, should be considered as a synonym for *to work*.

I was democratic, everyone agreed.

Once again the advantages announced themselves to me. The Spanish Language had been invented in Spain, the Royal Academy of the Language was located in Madrid. The Academy seeks to instruct us, so we will not forget the words the Spaniards gave us after they left us bereft of our own. Olga has traveled frequently to the Mother Country on departmental business. And so, who knows. . . .

On the steps I met up with my students. They had already said hi to Olga, learned she was getting married, she was leaving, and if I accepted her proposal I'd be taking her place. I assumed they had thoroughly considered whether this would be better or worse for them, and then reached the eternal conclusion of the young: that the question is not so important and the answer will take care of itself.

If I were an eighteen-year-old student I would already have

forgotten Daniel, I thought, as Ana winked at me while dancing down the stairs.

On my way out of the building, the secretary intercepted me to say that the reporter who never got to interview Daniel now wanted me to answer some questions about the university's joint projects with the Writers Union.

While we were talking, a 1960s-model Harley-Davidson stopped directly in front of the street door, looking as if it had emerged from an *Easy Rider* publicity still.

A tall boy stepped off, dressed all in black, carrying his helmet in one hand and a hibiscus flower in the other. Ana ran to him, hugged him, and kissed him again and again. Her friends came over to greet the boy, who smiled steadily while stroking Ana's hair.

The two of them got on the cycle and Ana said goodbye to her friends, the secretary, and me. The Harley-Davidson left, as if driving into the sunset, The End.

MANY YEARS AFTER THE war, after hunger, corpses, camps, marriages, separations, divorces, books . . . he had called. It's me. She had recognized his voice. It's me . . . His voice trembled, and that's when she recognized the accent.
                                                    —Marguerite Duras, *The North China Lover*

I WAS STANDING IN the corner of the bedroom next to the answering machine. When the phone rang, as always, I didn't lift the receiver. I waited, while my heartbeat sped up.

It was Daniel.

He was speaking with a new accent. The one that belongs to those who have tamed their Cuban inflections to lean toward that more pure-blooded speech. With the receiver in my hands, but still mute, I leaned back into the junction of the two walls and slid into a sitting position.

A braver Marian answered, saying something so absurd that

it made him laugh. His laugh was the same as always—engulfing my body, filling the room with sound as if the sea had come crashing in. His way of enjoying me as he enjoyed everything. My way of loving you, Daniel, because you were everything and I wanted to be everything for you.

I couldn't disguise my nervousness. I wanted to tell him that in those endless months I had done nothing but think about him. Or that in spite of everything, I still thought about him.

To tell him: Come over right now, I'm dying to see you, for you to touch me, to tell me what maybe you've forgotten but I repeated to myself every night. Or not to tell him anything, while making clear that I'm dying to.

But it was hard to say any of this to someone who had come back as a voice with a foreign accent. So I asked the question one asks in such situations. He answered that he'd been in town for quite a while and soon he'd explain why he'd taken so long to call. I told him he didn't need to explain anything.

"When can we see each other?" I asked, looking at the clock.

"About one, if you'll invite me to eat."

My brain began to function after a long idle time. I said yes, while recalling the phone numbers of two *paladares* that delivered Chinese food.

I would buy beer, because the weather was so hot. Cristal was the brand he liked. And I would buy ice cream. And coffee, a good brand that wouldn't clog the espresso pot. And some mild cigarettes. Lucky Strikes would do. The gas station on the corner would have all of that for sale, in dollars. This took me only a few seconds to plan.

"I'll expect you."

"I expect so. You haven't changed." I couldn't tell whether that was a question or a statement.

"Yes I have. I'm a mess," I answered, as if that were something I was happy about.

At six o'clock, the table had a resigned expression suggesting knowledge that it was not about to experience elbows, crumbs, or any sort of stain. I didn't cover the untouched serving dishes, or clear away the clean plates, glasses, and knives, and forks. I didn't remove the spotless tablecloth. I didn't light up a virgin Lucky Strike or open a can of lukewarm beer. While I searched for my bag, my keys, the door, and a destination in the city, I thought about my dead mother, solitude, days gone by and things lost. About Daniel, and about the time for waiting being over.

The phone rang and I heard Sergio's voice leaving a message. During the war in Iraq, seven thousand archaeological sites have been looted. In that crusade, which is sweeping away the most ancient of what we are, the original volume of *The Arabian Nights* has been destroyed.

Havana-Montagnola
October 2006–September 2008

ABOUT THE AUTHOR

Mylene Fernández-Pintado's novels have won the Italo Calvino Prize and Cuba's Critics' Award. Her short stories appear in anthologies in Cuba and abroad, and have been translated into English, French, Italian and German. She currently divides her time between Havana, Cuba and Lugano, Switzerland. This is her first complete work to appear in English.

ABOUT THE TRANSLATOR

Dick Cluster is a writer and translator based in Oakland, California. His original work includes three novels and two books of history, most recently *The History of Havana* (with Rafael Hernández). Other Cuban writers he has translated include Aida Bahr, Pedro de Jesús, and Abel Prieto.